DARK FLOOD

DARK
FLOOD

DARK FLOOD

KARON ALDERMAN

Orion

ORION CHILDREN'S BOOKS

First published in Great Britain in 2024 by Hodder & Stoughton

1 3 5 7 9 10 8 6 4 2

A CIP catalogue record for this book
is available from the British Library.

ISBN 978 1 510 10911 7

Typeset in Stymie BT by
Palimpsest Book Production Ltd, Falkirk, Stirlingshire

Printed and bound in Great Britain by
Clays Ltd, Elcograf S.p.A.

The paper and board used in this book
are made from wood from responsible sources.

MIX
Paper | Supporting
responsible forestry
FSC® C104740

Orion Children's Books
An imprint of
Hachette Children's Group
Part of Hodder & Stoughton Limited
Carmelite House
50 Victoria Embankment
London EC4Y 0DZ

An Hachette UK Company
www.hachette.co.uk

www.hachettechildrens.co.uk

For all those who keep trying.

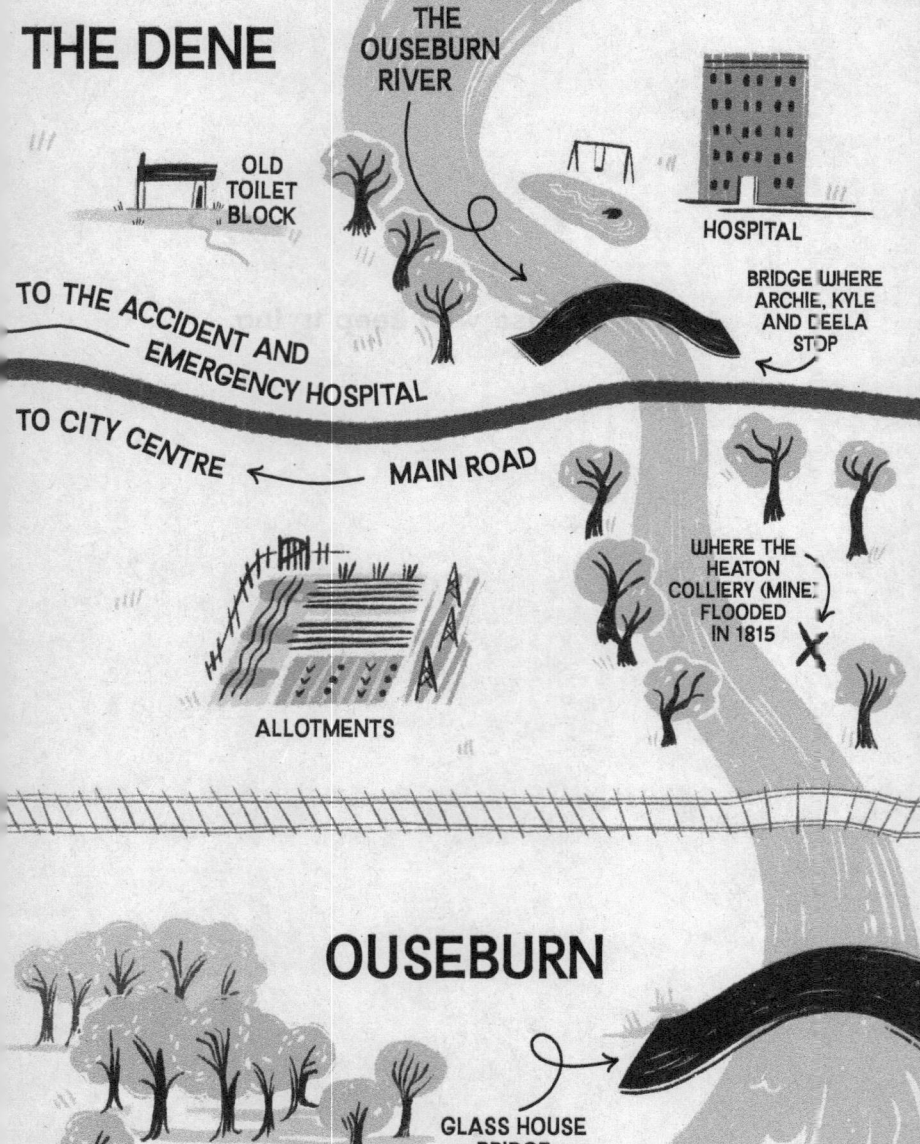

THE DENE

THE OUSEBURN RIVER

OLD TOILET BLOCK

HOSPITAL

TO THE ACCIDENT AND EMERGENCY HOSPITAL

BRIDGE WHERE ARCHIE, KYLE AND DEELA STOP

TO CITY CENTRE ← MAIN ROAD

WHERE THE HEATON COLLIERY (MINE) FLOODED IN 1815

ALLOTMENTS

OUSEBURN

GLASS HOUSE BRIDGE

RIVER TYNE

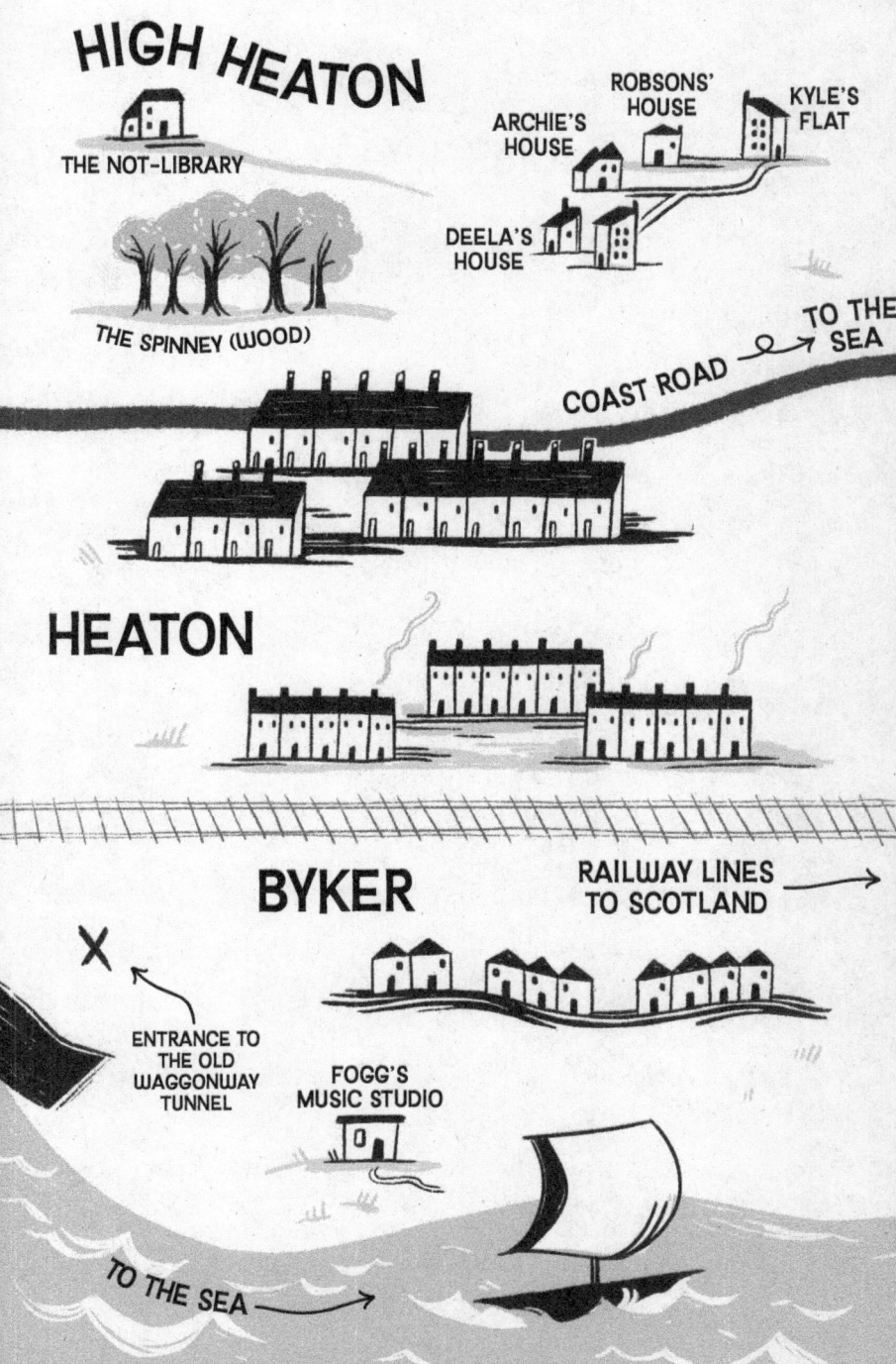

Dark watter's rising . . . a black flood, air so thick, like breathing blood. Shadows, monstrous in the gloom, dancin' on me grave . . . me hands, heavy now. 'Play for me lad,' I say. 'It eases the pain.'

A silver thread of tune, singin' me home.

1

The tall lad with the strange gadget is out in the Spinney again. He moves slowly through the trees, prodding the ground with his weird metal contraption. He doesn't look up as we pass.

'I bet he's one of them, you know, archaeologists.' Deela knows everything. I think of Granda sat in his chair, wheezing, watching people dig up old bones and swords and stuff and him, glued to the telly as they uncover the past.

'You gan on out, Archie,' he'd said. 'I'll have me nap. You gan out in the fresh air.'

So now, here's me and Kyle and Deela, just mooching around the estate, drifting through the scrubby little wood we call the

Spinney between our houses and the main road.

'What a waste of money,' Kyle says, fierce like, with a few swears sprinkled in like salt on chips. 'What we need round here is jobs, man, not diggin' up old history.'

I don't swear much, me, cos Mam goes radge and Granda says a real man doesn't need to use bad language. Kyle tries not to when he's with Granda, but he's got a short attention span, Kyle, and he forgets.

'Well, it's give him a job,' Deela says. 'And I don't see any digging going on.' She looks back over her shoulder. The lad's scanning the ground between the trees with his machine, which looks like a cross between a Zimmer frame and a metal detector. A bright red rucksack is propped up against one of the trees.

'It uses sound waves so they can see what's under there without digging it up,' I say, stepping round some dog poo and carrying on through the trees. 'I saw it on one of Granda's history shows.'

'Bet it costs a bomb,' Kyle grumbles.

We walk towards the main road, past the library. Really, it's the Not-Library cos it got closed down in the cuts. As we pass, Kyle says what he always says:

'It's a brand-new building! Why would they close a brand-new building?!'

Me and Deela snort with laughter.

'You sound like your mam,' she says. How to calm Kyle down . . . not.

'No way!' he says, but he still goes off on one of his rants about the government and how he could do a better job himself blah blah blah.

We cross the pavement pitted with small grey gum blobs. I imagine some archaeologist guy in a hundred years scraping away the layers, like they do on telly, and finding this grey-white layer. A grey-white deposit, they'd call it, analysing it. Gum and spit. They'd think it's, like, some strange sacrificial offering, *They came here and mingled their own saliva with the Holy*

Gum and offered it to the gods so that . . .' I
could almost hear the voiceover, dead posh
like.

'Well?' Kyle is standing, hands on hips,
waiting. 'How much you got?'

We scrat about in our pockets and
manage two quid between us. We go into the
Co-op and roam the four short aisles. A
bottle of pop and some doughnuts, or a slab
of chocolate? We go for the doughnuts and
head out of the shop and down the hill.

Me and Kyle and Adila. But we call her
Deela. She got put with us for a Year Five
history project and we've been hanging out
ever since. Deela says she likes us cos we're
not judgemental. And that's true. I don't
mind she's always got to be right and they
don't care I still hang round with me Granda,
playing his old fiddle. He's taught me since I
was a little kid. I know it's not cool so I keep
quiet about it. I don't do school concerts, just
play at home. Deela says it's keeping up a
tradition. Kyle says it's me human right to be
a saddo if I want.

We pass the bus stop and school. Kyle's mouth is full of doughnut, but he's not done with the previous conversation. 'That lad's just wastin' his time,' he says, taking another from the pack. 'Cos there's nowt more to know about this boring place.'

I squish a bit of the white fleshy dough between me fingers and an ooze of red jam slips out. We're still mooching along, off the main road now. It's not like there's anywhere we've got to be; it's summer holidays and nowt to do but hang out. Deela rolls the doughnut packet up and squishes it into her pocket.

'Seventy-five trees in the Spinney, planted for seventy-five men and boys.' She likes history. 'Don't you think it's sad, Kyle? All them men and boys dying? Trapped in the mine right under our feet?'

Kyle shrugs, scuffing up some crisp packets on the path. 'I s'pose, but it's all in the past. Two hundred years gone and buried. And let's face it, there's a disaster a day if you need one.' He's licking the sugar off his fingers and wiping his hands on his jeans. I try to be on both sides so they won't get into another stupid row, even though I cannet see that any of it matters.

'Aye, it's sad,' I say. 'But we already know what happened; how the miners accidentally broke through the wall into the abandoned workings and got flooded. What can Gadget Guy add to that?'

'Gadget Guy,' Deela says. 'Good name.'

'You couldn't pay me to prod around the ground all day,' Kyle goes on. 'What's the point? Like, when Granda tells us stories that's interesting, but at school . . .' He shrugs and pulls at a bit of twig sticking out of someone's garden. He starts to strip the leaves off. 'I mean, history's all kings . . .' he drops a leaf, 'and wars . . .' he drops another leaf, 'and dates and . . . ugh.' Kyle's not daft, but school isn't really his happy place. He breaks the twig and drops it.

Deela frowns at him. 'It's important to know about the past,' she says. 'It totally shapes the future, right, Archie?'

We're crossing the big iron pedestrian bridge that arches out over the park in the Dene below. We stop halfway and rest our arms on the metal railings and stare down at the tops of the trees beneath us. From up here you can see where the Ouseburn River cuts through. It's hot today. I can hear kids playing and shouting as they go into the cold water. Me and Kyle used to go down there all the time when we were little, with Granda minding us while Mam worked and Kyle's mam did whatever she did when she wasn't around.

'D'you remember when Granda used to let us play in the river, Kyle?' I say.

He nods. 'Aye, and he used to lift us both up and swing us round dead fast? Epic.'

'How is Granda?' Deela asks.

'Same,' I shrug. 'Bit low. He hates not being able to get out down the park and the allotments.' I think of him stuck in the house, wheezing away, his lungs and heart shutting down slowly. 'He's got this thing – *em-fa-seem-a*,' I say. 'It's where his lungs got damaged when he was working in the mines. It slowly gets worse and worse. Now he can't barely get out of his chair.' I stare out over the park so they cannet see me face.

'Why doesn't he get one of them scooters that old gadgies drive about in?' Kyle asks. 'Then he could get out a bit.'

'Dunno,' I say. 'I think they're, like, massively expensive.' I don't mention my dad, cos there'll be no help from him. We all kind of pretend he doesn't exist cos that's easier than admitting the guy is a scumball who took off and left us – me, Granda and Mam. He never sends us anything, never mind money. I've not even heard from him in ages. Two years, mebbes? I dunno. Don't want to either. Mam thinks he rings me now and then. So the truth is I lie to her sometimes.

Kyle kicks at an empty can, sending it right across the wide pathway. 'Money, cash, dosh, loot, dough – that's lots of names for summat you never get to see.' His voice changes. 'Hey! Why don't we, like, raise the money?'

10

Deela doesn't shoot him down like she usually does. Instead, she twirls the end of her plait round her finger. She does that when she's thinking. 'We'd need to do some research,' she says. 'Find out how much . . . but we could start. Oh, we could do cake sales! My cousin did that so she could go to Peru when she was in Year Eleven with school. She says homemade samosas go like hot-cakes.'

'She must've sold a ship load of samosas,' Kyle adds, grinning.

'Well, you got any better ideas?' Deela sounds huffy.

'I'm thinking,' Kyle says. He's always got big money-making ideas but somehow they never turn into actual money.

'What about a litter pick?' Deela says, searching 'mobility scooters' on her phone as she's talking. 'There's enough of it round here. We could get sponsored.'

'Nobody's got any money,' I say. 'Not the kind of money we'd need.'

11

'Wow,' she says. 'Yeah, we are talking four figures here. But you can get them cheaper on eBay. Second-hand.'

'I still don't think we could make anywhere near enough. Plus, no one wants to take on kids our age for jobs anyway.' I take a few steps back and start moving off the bridge. I don't want to talk about it any more. I hate thinking about how poorly Granda is now.

Kyle and Deela follow me down towards the park gates. It's halfway through the summer holidays and our feet just walk the same old route without us thinking or talking about it. We head into Pets Corner like we're kids again. A gran with a little lad in a red hoodie gives us a funny look, as if we're gonna bring trouble. Old people always think teenagers are trouble – except Granda – it's like he remembers what it's like being young. Kyle reads the labels on the cages out loud, putting on different voices for each animal.

'Hi, I'm a Nubian goat,' Kyle says in a strong Scottish accent. 'I guess I come from Nubia.' He thinks for a moment. 'Archie,' he says, turning to me. 'Where the bl—' Deela coughs loudly and nudges him, '—the hell is Nubia?' He finishes.

The gran frowns and moves the kid on to the next animal pen.

'You shouldn't swear in front of little kids,' Deela tells him.

'"Hell" isn't swearing,' he says, surprised.

She giggles. The Nubian goat shakes its long ears, turns its back on us and shows us its bum.

'I know!' Kyle says. 'We could make some money busking!'

I look at him blankly.

'Where did *that* come from? You see a goat's bum and you think "busking"? I dunno how your brain works, man.'

13

He stares at the goats, not looking at me. His ears are starting to go red.

'For Granda, for the scooter. I was just thinking about Nubia – how can there be a country I've never even heard of? I bet it's a dead poor place.'

Deela sits on a bench and leans back in the sun. Kyle carries on, still staring at the goat which is dropping a pile of poo. He must be thinking dead hard cos he doesn't even mention it.

'So then I was thinking it's rubbish being poor. Lads can make money busking. I've seen them performers in town and they aren't anywhere near as good as you, Archie. But people just give them money!'

'Yeah, to go away!' Deela adds, but Kyle isn't joking around. It's the first time he's said I'm a good player, ever.

'And it was Granda who taught you, so it all works out,' he adds. 'It's like . . . payback for all them lessons and stuff. I'd do it only I cannet sing or play or anything.' Deela grins. We both remember Kyle trying out the trumpet in Year Five. It was horrible. 'I've thought it all out,' he's talking fast now, words falling over each other. 'I could be, like, your minder and mind the money and stop people beating you up.'

'Thanks for that,' I say. Kyle is tiny – a small blond skinny kid with a shaven head. He looks like a naked mole-rat in glasses. *Not* an obvious bodyguard.

'What about me?' Deela says, miffed that she's not been included.

'What could you do?' Kyle says, tactless as ever. 'Anyway, your dad wouldn't let you go and stand with two lads busking in town, would he?'

She's silent again, but it's a thinking silence.

'He might not find out,' she says finally.

2

We're wandering along kicking the idea around like an old football. Kyle's trying to convince us to go busking and I'm thinking of a hundred reasons not to. Numbers one to a hundred being: if you don't want to get picked on, don't stand in a public space and play a fiddle.

We turn the corner and there's a group of lads hanging out by the locked-up toilet block. Some are sitting on an old bench and there's a vape haze round them. A lad with red hair is leaning against the wall.

'Uh-oh,' Deela murmurs. It's one of them Robson twins.

'And where there's one, there's two,' I say.

I glance sideways at Kyle and his face is fixed and blank. You cannet smile or look like you're having a good time cos them lads take it personal.

Tyler Richards is there as well, sat on his bike pretending to be a big man even though he's a year younger than us – just a kid, really. He takes off and does a lap almost up to us and back. As he whizzes past he gives a sudden yell that makes us all jump.

'I *hate* that,' Deela says, under her breath.

Me mouth's dry and me face feels hot. I try not to look at them. The other Robson twin comes out from behind the old toilet block with something flat and black in his hand.

'Hey, Brad, what d'you think this is worth? Catch!' It's Robson One – the one that does all the yelling. That's the only way you can tell them apart. He grins, tossing a slim iPad to his brother. It misses and smashes to the ground. 'Oy!' he yells at Tyler. 'Pick it up then!' Like it was his fault in the first place.

Tyler scrambles off his bike, picks up the iPad and passes it to Robson Two.

We are so nearly past them, trying to keep out of it, but then Robson One spots us.

'Who are yous looking at?' he shouts and moves to block our way.

Deela stiffens but doesn't look away. He stares at her and she stares back.

'What you doin' with them losers?' he says like he owns the place, even though the twins only moved here two months back.

Deela doesn't answer.

'D'you like it? Me dad give it me.' He grins, holding the iPad out to her. We all know his dad's in prison, and if it was really his I doubt he'd be hoying it around like it didn't matter if it smashed. 'You can have it if you want . . . I could do you a *special* deal.' He looks at his mates and they all echo his laugh. It's not *what* he says, it's the way he says it – loaded. I edge closer to Deela, look back the way we came but Robson Two's silently blocking the path behind us.

Kyle takes his glasses off like he's expecting trouble.

Deela raises an eyebrow. 'You can keep it,' she says and just keeps walking. Robson One finally steps back and lets her through.

'It's not yours, is it?' Kyle says, like it's just occurred to him. There's another belch of laughter from the group. I can't help it, I look up, straight into Robson One's eyes. His whole attention focuses on me.

'What you lookin' at?' He moves in close, staring. It's like looking into the eyes of a wolf. 'You want to be careful, you do. What are you lot anyway, neighbourhood watch? Eyeing our place all the time with your nebby old granda starin' out the window, sticking his nose in other people's business.'

Me teeth are clenched so tight me jaw hurts. It's like we freeze-frame. It's probably two seconds, but it feels way longer.

Suddenly there's a whole pack of barking dogs racing across the grass, and behind them four large middle-aged women in bright T-shirts chatting away like the world is normal.

Robson One nods his head to the others and they all take off, loping away the way we'd come. He turns and shouts, 'Losers!'

The women with the dogs don't even notice. It's like we're not on their radar at all.

We walk as fast as we can in the opposite direction to the Robsons. As soon as the path twists and we're out of sight, we run up the steep bank covered in trees and bushes all hanging off the cliff of the Dene.

'I could definitely win against one of them,' Kyle says, putting his glasses back on His face has gone red. I'm not sure if it's just heat or if he knows he's lying. 'If I could just take them one at a time.'

'Well, they're joined at the hip, so no luck with that,' I say.

'They give us the creeps,' Deela says. 'Every time they see me and Nabila in the street they give us hacky looks. I dunno know why they hate us.'

'They hate everyone,' I say. 'They're just messing with us because they can.'

The path comes to a sudden end in a mass of rock and mud. I crawl under the wire fencing off where the landslide came down in the winter and the others follow. Deela stops talking so she can concentrate on picking her way across the fallen branches and deep cracks in the ground. It's all dry now, and the rocks and mud lie in a tangle of roots and dead twigs. You'd not know there'd even been a path. We scramble up the bank and sit in what's become our secret place, hidden from sight by the weeds and bushes. Kyle turns round and round like he's a dog making a den, then sort of slumps down.

Deela pulls her knees up against her chin and stares out over the treetops. She groans. 'We should tell somebody about that iPad.'

'We don't actually know it's nicked,' I say. 'Could be a broken one and he's just messing with our heads.'

'We totally need to train up,' Kyle adds, 'in case they, like, surprise us.'

'Get real,' I say. As if Kyle could take them anyway. 'No training up. Just ignore them. And it's not true about Granda watching them – he just likes to look outside. It's not like he can help seeing their place, given they live right opposite us!'

Deela twirls the fluffy end of her plait. 'Yeah, with the garden they've turned into a junkyard. Dad says they're bringing the estate down.' She sighs. 'Why did they have to move *here*?'

I pick up a stone and toss it from hand to hand. 'I heard their mam wants a fresh start for them.' I throw it into the green tangle of undergrowth, hear it bouncing down the hill. 'At our school.'

Kyle swears quietly. Deela shakes her head.

There's a long silence that isn't really silence. Birds are making that shout-shouting noise birds make. There's the sound of kids playing, a siren in the distance and the hum of traffic on the roads round the park.

'How about tomorrow?' Kyle suddenly says.

I have no idea what he's on about.

'The buskin', Archie, man,' he says, like he's already forgotten about the Robsons. 'So we can get that scooter. We owe Granda that much, don't we? No time like the present.'

Me stomach lurches a bit. Don't get me wrong, a mobility scooter's a good idea. Granda could motor down the park and sit in the sun, mebbes get back to being himself. But I've never played the fiddle in front of a load of strangers. It's something me and Granda share, almost like it's private. I've only ever played for him and Mam, Kyle and Deela. And I played for Dad before he left. Mebbe that's why he left. He hated us playing that fiddle.

'What's that sound?' Deela says suddenly. I can hear a scrabbling noise.

I jump up, pulling her with me, ready to run from the Robsons.

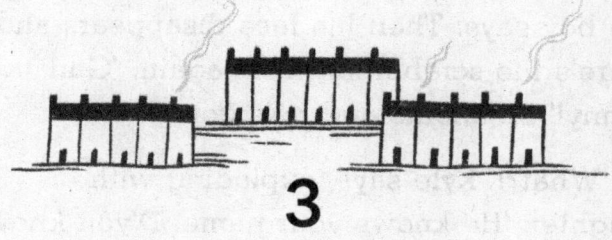

3

'Howay, lads!' a voice calls.

We look up and see a boy hanging off the side of the cliff like a monkey, peering out of the bushes. His thin face is streaked with dirt. I've never seen him before in me life – he's definitely not from our school.

'Howay!' he says, looking straight at me. 'Gan away, yem – yer needed at yer hoose.'

'Who the hell are you?' Kyle says.

'You shouldn't be hanging off the cliff,' Deela says. 'You'll bring the whole lot down. You can see it's not stable!'

'Bossy,' Kyle mutters, but under his breath so she doesn't hear and get radgy.

'Archie! Away home, man! Yer wanted,' the boy says. Then his face disappears and there's the scrabbling noise again. 'Gan canny!' he shouts and he's gone.

'What?!' Kyle says, exploding with laughter. 'He knows your name. D'you know him?'

'Nah,' I say. 'Someone must've put him up to it, for a joke, like.'

'Weirdo,' Deela adds. 'It's not much of a joke, is it? D'you suppose he's been listening in on us? Spying on us for the Robsons?'

'Doesn't look like one of their mates.' I know he's probably just messing on, but suddenly I feel there's something dead important I should be doing – somewhere else I need to be. I scramble to me feet. 'I better get home anyways. Mam said to keep an eye on Granda and he'll be needin' a cup of tea.' I'm moving as I speak and the others swap a look, but they follow.

It only takes a moment to climb to the top of the hill. Then we're out of the wild park with the landslips and the tangled trees and on to a grassy football field with a play area, all very tame and neat. Normally we'd hang out on the swings, getting hacky looks off the mams with little kids, but today there's this strange fear in me belly and I want to get home so bad, the others can't hardly keep up with me.

As we come down the main road to our estate I start to run, and it's like Deela and Kyle catch the panic and they run n'all. We shoot past the Not-Library and pound along the street. I struggle with the key, which always sticks a bit, and we crash into the house feeling like all that urgency was for nowt.

'Granda?' I call, feeling dead stupid. He'll be sat in front of the telly like usual, of course he will. I can hear it talking away to itself. 'Granda?' I shout again, knowing that he can't shout back, that his voice is just a thin whisper now. I go into the sitting room. He's lying back in his chair, eyes closed, his face this strange blue-grey colour.

'No!' Deela shouts.

I run to him and grab his hand – he's still warm. There's a sudden rasp of breath.

'He's breathing,' I say. 'Granda, hold on, man, hold on.' I start talking to him. I don't know what I'm saying, just any old crap so he'll know he's not on his own.

'Eurgh . . . eurgh . . . dark!' he says and draws that terrible rasping breath again.

'Ring an ambulance!' I shout, but Kyle's already on it.

Deela gently moves Granda's head to try and open up his airway, and I pull his oxygen mask over his face and hold his hand. I hated that stupid mask and tank of oxygen when he first got it, but now I'm glad there's something I can do that'll help. I slide me fingers across his knobbly knuckles, feeling the cords and bones of the hand that taught me how to hold the bow, how to find the notes. Now it's limp. I give it a gentle squeeze but he doesn't squeeze back.

'They're sendin' an ambulance,' Kyle says, listening to the voice on the phone. 'Keep him warm,' he adds. 'She says keep him warm.'

Deela runs and grabs my duvet from my room and we tuck it round him.

'Kyle, you go and open the front door for them,' she says. 'I'll ring your mam, Archie.' She grabs my phone and dials. 'She's not picking up,' Deela says after a minute, whispering 'Come on, come on, pick up!' as she redials.

Kyle moves slowly to the door and hovers there – half in the room, half in the hallway – hanging on to the door frame like he cannet stand up by himself. He's staring at Granda.

'Who was that weird lad in the park?' he asks suddenly. 'How did he *know*?'

I stroke Granda's hand. I can't even think about it.

'I dunno,' I say, 'but whoever he is, I owe him one.'

4

Deela's holding Granda's hand and I'm adjusting his oxygen mask when I hear the siren. I rush past Kyle and nearly fall over him trying to get down the hall to open the door. Two paramedics, a tall guy and a short woman, climb out of the ambulance.

'He's in the front room,' I say. 'Me Granda. I give him oxygen and he's sort-of breathing. He's got this lung problem . . . will he be OK?' Me hands are shaking.

'What's his name?' the man says.

'Bill,' I say. 'Er, William Bell, but nobody calls him that.' The man nods.

The para goes straight into the front room while the other pulls a bag from the

30

ambulance. I turn to go back to Granda when Gadget Guy from the Spinney comes powering up the street looking like he's in a right radge. He glances at the ambulance and hesitates, then calls to me.

'Hey! Did you see a tall red-headed boy round here?' He pushes his hands through his dark curly hair. His voice is loud and posh. 'He nicked my rucksack this morning! I actually saw him take it but he ran off. I've just seen him again coming through the alley. D'you know him?'

Kyle's right behind us. 'It's OK, Archie. I've got this.' He turns to Gadget Guy. 'Aye, it's one of the Robson twins,' he says enthusiastically, pointing at the house opposite. 'They live there – the one with all the junk in the garden.'

'*Kyle!*' I try and push his hand down, but it's too late. There's a flicker of movement at the window across the road. Great. Kyle's been me best mate forever but he's not the brightest spark. He'd go through flood and fire to save us. He probably wouldn't survive and I'd die with him, but not for lack of trying. He just never thinks things through. And now not only has he just dobbed us in, but someone has definitely seen. And that cannet be good.

'Look,' I say to Gadget Guy, 'we've got stuff going on.' I wave me hand towards the ambulance.

Gadget Guy nods like he understands, but he doesn't move. 'I'll tell the police the name – Robson. I still can't believe it . . .'

The Robsons' window is open and whoever moved those curtains will hear every word of his loud, confident voice and will think we're mates with him, helping him dob them into the police.

'Kyle,' I say, low as I can. 'Are they watching us?'

Kyle shrugs and turns his back on the Robsons' house like he believes if he can't see them, they cannet see him.

'Kyle!' I say louder. 'Get him out of me garden!' I go back into the front room where the paramedics are checking Granda over and Deela is telling them everything I should be telling them.

'I can't get my head round how that boy in the park played that pathetic joke on us,' she's saying, 'and then it turned out good. Oh, here's Archie – he'll know all Granda's medication.'

'Tell Kyle to get rid of Gadget Guy,' I hiss, then run and grab Granda's pills from the bedroom. I knock down his box of tissues, his pile of old history books and his glass of water but I ignore the mess and race back to give them to one of the paras.

'Archie, do you have anyone else living here? Any adults apart from your Granda?' the woman asks. She's got a kind face and a tattoo of a sunflower on her arm.

I'm about to explain we've not managed to get hold of Mam when me phone rings. For a minute I scrat around trying to find it. I dunno what the hell I'm doing apart from panicking. Deela grabs it off the chair where she'd left it and answers the call. She holds it out to me, but I shake me head. I cannet tell her.

Deela puts the phone to her ear. 'Mrs Bell?'

There's this weird silence where Mam must be asking what's going on.

'Archie's OK. It's Granda. We've called an ambulance. They're taking him to . . .' she looks at the paramedics.

'The Royal Victoria,' one says.

Deela repeats it to Mam. She listens for a bit and I can hear Mam's voice twittering in the distance. Deela makes them sounds girls are good at – soothing, like. She disconnects and hands me back the phone. 'She says she'll meet you there.'

The paras have got Granda strapped on to a stretcher. He's still unconscious. I can hear Kyle and Gadget Guy in the hallway now, still talking. *Not* what I meant when I told Kyle to get him out of me garden.

I open the sitting room door, wide as I can, so's the paras can get the stretcher out.

Gadget Guy is filling the hall. 'I just turned my back on it – literally five minutes!'

Kyle's shifting from one foot to the other like he's got ants in his trainers. 'It would've been funny if your phone had been in the rucksack they took.' He's talking really fast – motor-mouth Kyle that gets wrong at school for not shutting up. 'Well, not funny like ha-ha, just kind of weird funny . . . Sort of ironic funny cos you'd not be able to phone cos your phone would've been gone.'

If Kyle doesn't stop talking soon, I'll explode.

The paras wheel the stretcher out into the hall, Granda looking grey and limp.

'God, I'm so sorry,' Gadget Guy says, like he's only just realised this is an emergency. 'I'll go,' he says, like he's doing me a favour. Kyle pushes the front door wide and they stand on the front path, as the paras gently move the stretcher out on to the pavement.

As they start loading Granda into the ambulance he opens his eyes, just for a moment.

'Please,' I say to the paras, 'I need to go with him. He'll not know what's happening.'

The para says I can if I keep out of the way. I climb in and at the last minute remember to shout to Deela to lock up the house. I get one last look back. She and Kyle and Gadget Guy are on the front path, staring after us – like they've not quite realised the show is over – before the paramedic swings the door shut and the ambulance pulls away.

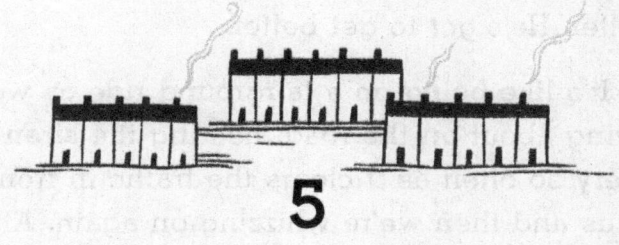

5

The ambulance rocks slightly and I'm on this
high, slippy seat, feeling weird. Granda looks
kind of small now, much smaller than he
used to. I stretch over to stroke his hand,
watch him struggling for each breath.

'He'll not die?' I ask, and me voice sounds
all high, like a girl's voice.

'Not if we can help it,' the para says,
adjusting the oxygen mask.

Granda suddenly grips me hand, just for a
moment, and I know he'll not give in without
a fight. *I'll get that money for the scooter*, I
think. It doesn't matter if I hate playing in
front of people; Granda doesn't deserve to
never get out in the sun again. It's his fiddle
and he taught me, so it's only right I use it

to get him a bit of freedom for when he gets better. He's *got* to get better.

It's like being on a fairground ride as we swing about on the road, hearing the siren every so often as it clears the traffic in front of us and then we're whizzing on again. Any other time it would be cool to just carve your way across the city, sirens screaming and doing that *whup, whup whupper whupper* thing when cars don't get out the road fast enough. But not today, not when every extra minute feels like torture. We live dead near a hospital but we have to get across the city to a *different* hospital with an Accident and Emergency, which feels crazy and gives me too much time to watch him trying to breathe. I try to think calm stuff.

I imagine taking out the fiddle. Nobody makes me play it for two hours a day, nobody tells me what to do or gives me stars on a chart. It's just something I've always done, ever since I watched Granda playing. I wanted so bad to be able to play like him. I imagine it in me hands, the wood warm like a live creature. It's dead old, really, stained and chipped like it's fit for the bin. But it's Granda's and I'd never want another.

When I was little, he would let me get it out of its case and bring it to him, sat at the table.

'He'll drop it,' Mam would warn. 'He's only little, he'll drop it.'

As if.

Granda would say, 'Hold it like this, Archie – see, your little arms aren't long enough yet. One day it'll fit you and then, when I'm gone, it'll be yours. Remember that, right? Your dad's never had time for it, so it's you it'll come to. It's been in the family a long time. Me father gave it me, showed me how to play and his father gave it him. The fiddle's in your blood, lad.'

And then he'd play me tunes and I'd follow him on a little tiny fiddle Mam hired from a shop in town. He showed me where to put me fingers and how to drag the bow across.

'Like a cat bein' skinned,' Mam had said, but she let me keep at it and she was dead proud when I played a tune that really sounded like itself.

'That's "Twinkle Twinkle"!' she'd said, amazed. Aye, right, a tune's meant to sound like itself. And then I slowly learned all the songs Granda played, but the little hired fiddle never sounded like his. It didn't sing out with the same rich sound. I couldn't wait for me arms to grow, like I hadn't heard what he'd said. I hadn't heard the bit about him being gone.

'Here we are,' the para says as we drive into the hospital gates. They start shifting Granda out. I try to hold his hand, but I just get in the way.

'Archie!' Mam's running across the waiting area looking red and stressed out and still in her uniform from the bakery. She grabs me in a big, hot, sweaty hug.

'He'll be OK,' she says. 'They'll make him better.' She's always dead optimistic. 'I'm so glad you were home, or who knows what might've happened . . .'

We hang around the hospital for hours. I wish I could thank that lad in the park – even if it was his idea of a joke. While I'm waiting, I get a ton of messages from Kyle and Deela asking after Granda. Seems they took Gadget Guy to Deela's house, and her mam's giving him cups of tea and sympathy. I roll me eyes. What a load of fuss for just a rucksack!

It's hard to think about anything that's not here and now, sitting listening to the hum of lights and machines and hearing people coming and going on the other side of the cubicle curtain. I stroke Granda's hand gently – the one without the tube taped to it. I stare at his face. He looks like a zombie but his breathing's a bit better with the bigger mask on. His eyes suddenly open and watch me, confused like, as if he can't work out how he got here.

41

We wait. Different nurses come and go and Mam whispers with them in the corner of the cubicle. Then we wait some more while they move Granda up on to a ward. Mam and me go up to check he's settled and OK. The ward is a long corridor, with rooms off it, full of old men with tubes coming out of their noses, like elephant trunks, and out of their skinny purple hands. Mam pulls the curtains round Granda's bed so we can be private. It's so hot I can barely breathe, but there's this smell that makes me feel like I don't really want to. Granda looks all shrunk down in the big hospital bed. I hate the thought of leaving him here; I want to just stay with him for as long as it takes, but Mam promises we'll come back tomorrow. We hold his hands until he falls asleep. The sun is setting as we wait at the bus stop to get back across to our side of the city.

*

Me and Mam have only been home about twenty minutes when Kyle turns up on the doorstep, which is good cos he interrupts our row. Mam wants me to ring Dad and tell him about Granda.

She bangs some cheese on toast on the table and turns her back on us, fussing around with the kettle. I think she's crying but Kyle doesn't notice.

'Deela cannet come out – her dad says he doesn't want her "roaming the streets in the evening". Dunno what's the difference. What does he think she might do in the evening she wouldn't do in the day? And when does day turn into evening?' Kyle says 'evening' like it's a swear word. 'Anyway, for tomorrow, me and Deela have got it all planned out.' He's dead excited, like he always is when he's started a new project or got a scheme going. He turns to Mam suddenly. 'Is Granda getting better now he's in the hospital? He'll be out soon, won't he?'

Mam doesn't turn round so I nod instead. He's got to, right?

Kyle perks up. 'Planning, Archie, you know, the . . .' he does a funny action with his hands, like he's driving a scooter. He probably thinks Mam won't approve. Most adults don't approve of Kyle's ideas.

Mam gets the milk out, then leans against the fridge looking tired.

'He's settled on the ward and they've sorted his oxygen levels out. Howay then, Kyle, help eat up some of that cheese on toast. I don't fancy it now.' She pushes a packet of biscuits at us both. 'And yous can have these. I'm going for a quick shower.' She doesn't look at us, probably cos she's still mad that I won't ring Dad about what's happened. I dunno why I cannet bring myself to tell her I don't even know where he is, or that I've not even heard from him in two years. Or that the last number I had for him doesn't work any more . . .

Me and Kyle munch away at the cheese on toast, only it doesn't seem to taste of anything and it sticks in me throat as I swallow. Kyle eats Mam's, then finishes off my second piece.

'That's good, that is. Mam's stopped buying cheese now she's doing Veganuary all year round – I kind of miss it.' He scrapes the crumbs and little bits of melted cheese up off his plate. 'Sooo good. You could package these and sell them. Call 'em crispy cheese crumbs . . . toasty cheese crumbs . . . or choasties?'

For once it's good Kyle is making noise. The house seems so quiet without the telly going and Granda's rasping breath.

'I need a bit of air,' I say and we grab a handful of biscuits each and go out into the dark. The city feels hot and still, like it's under a thick black blanket. 'They'll be moving him from emergency to the local hospital tomorrow,' I tell Kyle. 'Seems the lung department's this side of the city.'

'Crazy!' Kyle says. 'They'll have to stick him in another ambulance and bring him all the way back again. What's the point in that?!'

I laugh. It's good to hear Kyle rant, it makes things feel normal.

We follow the same route we took earlier today, our feet carving out a path that our

45

brains don't even think about. Only now it's dark and the trees cast black shapes on the grey pavement. The orange glow of streetlights barely reaches down into the steep valley of the park. I can hear the river and the rustle of birds and small animals – likely rats round here. This is what the city used to be like, all dark and secret.

Granda sometimes talked about when he started work, way back in the 1960s, going from one mine to the next as they gradually all closed down. But he mostly liked to tell us the stories about miners from hundreds of years back. 'Under our feet,' he'd say. 'All them tunnels and passages are still there under the ground, abandoned.' The Engine Pit, Heaton Banks, Heaton High Main, Killingworth – I loved hearing all the names. He told us about men inventing steam engines to pump water out the pits, and how men and boys went down in the darkness for up to eighteen hours a day. Some were just little kids, mebbe only six or seven years old. When Granda talked we could feel what it was like – something terrible but somehow awesome as well.

I stop and lean against the bridge railings, looking down on to the top of the trees just like we did earlier before everything kicked off. Only it feels like a different place now, dark and quiet, and Granda's not at home but in the hospital with tubes and lights and machines beeping. How can so much have changed in a day? Here, there's no sound of kids and even the traffic's gone quieter. There's not a breath of air in the city tonight. I can see some of the bushes moving, though. I wonder if it's a fox. We saw one a few years back, creeping along with a pigeon in its mouth. I try to think about when Granda's better. A scooter would get him out and about and he'd be himself again, just on wheels instead of legs.

Kyle must be thinking about Granda, too, because he says, 'D'you remember when we used to come down here after school? Granda used to pick us up and bring us with a bag full of jam stotties?'

I laugh. 'Aye, and Mam went radge cos I wrecked me school shoes when I fell in the river.'

47

'Remember how we climbed that massive tree and all the mams with little kids were screaming, telling us to come down before we fell?'

'And Granda just said "leave them be, they're canny little climbers". And we were good, weren't we?' I can feel we're both grinning in the dark.

'So,' Kyle says. 'Whatever it costs, right?' And I know he's not talking about the past any more. He lets me in on his master plan. 'Tomorrow, right? No point waiting. We'll get up dead early – like, nine-ish – and then go to Monument in town and just do it. Deela's said she'll come n'all. We'll be like your minders.'

Only it's me everyone'll be looking at. I don't say anything, though.

'I bet we make a ton of money,' Kyle says, words tumbling out quickly. 'We've got two weeks of the summer holiday left – shame we didn't think of it sooner. But if we go every day I bet we could get one for when he comes home! Cash down – see their faces when you pull out a massive bag of dough!'

I don't want to put a downer on Kyle's plans, but it reminds me of when he tried to sell water bombs in school. That was gonna make a ton of money too – I mean, as he said, who doesn't want a water bomb? The teachers, it turned out.

The adrenaline of the day's making me antsy, like I cannet settle. The river glints down below, winding its way through the woods at the bottom of the valley. I remember Granda walking us all the way to the River Tyne once. Seems a lifetime ago. I don't want to go home with him not there.

'Let's walk,' I say.

 6

We head off the bridge and go in the opposite direction to earlier, through the woods. The path is gloomy, a dark archway of trees around it like a tunnel.

'So,' I say, 'what happened with Gadget Guy? He was up a height given he only lost a rucksack.'

Kyle hunts through his pockets looking for a stray sweet or some gum but comes up empty. 'Howay, man, it had his iPad in it – worth about a thou, he said.'

I let out a whoosh of air. 'No wonder he was radgy, then. D'you think it was that one the Robsons were hoying about in the park? Are they that stupid?'

'Aye,' Kyle snorts. 'Probably have to share a brain. That's why only one of them does all the talking – Mr Main Robson One, AKA the mouth.'

'Right,' I add, getting on a roll. 'Not just one *brain*, mebbes they've only got one brain *cell* between them.' I mimic their voices. 'Hey Robson Two, let us have a lend of the brain cell, I need to find me own feet . . . Hey Robson One, the brain cell's not working, I cannet find me own mouth. I know . . .' I'm laughing really hard now I can barely speak and Kyle's hunched over, giggling. 'If Robson One's the mouth . . . then Robson Two's the other end – he's the—'

As I shout the punchline, two figures suddenly emerge from the darkness. For a moment I can only see movement, but there's something about the way they walk so close, the same gangly silhouettes not talking. I just know.

'It's *them*!' I whisper.

'Did they hear you?' Kyle murmurs back. He's poised to run but it's already too late.

They lope towards us. One goes straight past and I think they've not recognised us. Mebbe they didn't hear what I just said. But the other stops dead, blocking the path. He laughs like someone's given him a present.

'Me favourite lads,' he says. 'Doin' stand-up now, eh?'

We turn to run but the path is blocked behind us by the other twin.

Robson One steps closer to us. I can smell him – a sickly mix of sweat and vape. 'Double act. Sooo funny.' He smacks his fist against his hand and I flinch at the noise. 'Yous grassed on us earlier.'

We shake our heads but it's pointless. Me body feels like lead and me brain like it's on a treadmill gannin way too fast. Cannet tell a lie – he's got us nailed.

'What should we do with them, Brad?' he says.

A gob of spit sails past my ear – Robson Two's contribution. Suddenly me brain and legs connect. I grab Kyle's arm and he swings round, sliding on some gravel. We dive sideways into the thick bushes and go rolling down the steep hill. I stagger back on me feet and skid down the rest of the bank. A branch stabs me in the arm and I can hear Kyle crashing down nearby, swearing his head off. Brambles rip me T-shirt and skin. We roll out of the bushes on to the bottom path and leg it. Kyle sprints ahead of me towards a gateway to the lane next to the river and the allotments. We scramble over a wall and hide behind a shed.

We're both bent double, gasping and panting for air. I stare back into the darkness, but I cannet see them. 'They could be anywhere,' I whisper. We crouch down, listening to our own breathing, and both jump out of our skins as a bird flaps off with a startled shriek.

There's a shout from one of the twins in the distance and the other gives a fake wolf howl that makes the hairs on me arms stand up. Are they coming closer? I'm trying to stop me breathing giving us away. Kyle's crouched next to me, his eyes bugging out of his head.

The yells fade off, but they could be waiting. I can smell dirt and the green sap smell where the plants have been crushed and broken.

'Did they get me?' Kyle whispers, straining round to see if the gob has hit him. 'D'you think they'll kill me for telling Gadget Guy their names and where they live?'

'What do you think?!' I whisper back furiously. 'You grassed them up, pointing your big fat finger straight at their place. They must've seen you do it. It's not like they're gonna give you a polite handshake and a medal, is it?'

'Well, the police would know it was them anyways. I mean, it's not rocket science, is it? Gadget Guy says two tall ginger lads in the Spinney took his iPad. They'll know exactly who, won't they? Them lads've got track, man.'

'Aye, go on, you tell yourself that, but that's not the way them Robsons'll see it. Why couldn't you just stay out of it?'

He rubs his hands through the dirt, picking out some small stones. 'At least I didn't just make fun of them to their faces.'

'Whatever. Grass on lads like the Robsons you're like a dead man walking. Gadget Guy'll be gone in a few weeks but we have to live with them twins forever.' I know Kyle's right, but it's making me radgy. This day's just been too much and me brain's exploding.

Kyle squints at me in the dark. 'Until they get locked up,' he adds optimistically. He's not joking either. We sit on the dirt under a bush, like, forever, just in case the Robsons are waiting for us up at the top of the hill. The woods rustle and creak all around us. I can hear the rush of the water along the valley. I wipe the sweat out of me eyes.

A dog barks; there are footsteps moving away and the sound of distant sirens up on the main road. Finally, I've had enough of sitting in the dirt with me legs going numb.

'Howay,' I say. 'Keep movin'.' We start to jog the wrong direction to home hoping they can't be bothered to chase us all the way down river.

Neither of us stops until we get to the lane out of the valley, to houses and shops. We walk home along the main road in silence, just in case they're at the park gates or hanging out by the Co-op. It's a long way. When we finally come into the estate it's from the other end, so we pass Kyle's flat first.

'We're on for tomorrow, aren't we?' Kyle says at his gate. 'We are on for tomorrow? We're good, aye? Aren't we?'

I'm so tired I don't answer.

'I mean,' he adds, sounding pathetic, 'we want to get that scooter, don't we? We want to do it for Granda? Right?'

'Right. See you tomorrow, then,' I say grudgingly.

I peer round the corner. No sign of the Robsons. I run like a rabbit, key ready in me hand, and burst into the house.

7

The noise roars at me like a great, hot
lion.

'Get back, man,' I yell. 'Run for it!'

I sprint into the blackness. It's like I'm
running over spikes – where the hell are me
shoes? The path's littered with bits of rock
and nails, and I can feel sticky blood running
between me toes.

'Howay!' A voice says and a hand grabs
mine in the dark. 'Watch out, lads – gan up
the rise, the watter's coming! Hauld on!' It's a
familiar voice, but I can't think who. I take a
deep breath of the hot shadowy air.

BANG! BANG! BANG!

Me ears are cracking. I'm fighting to breathe, wrestling the duvet. Me eyes are still tight shut when I realise there's no blood, no darkness, but the banging's real. I groan, roll out of bed and stagger to the front door where Kyle is jiggling up and down impatiently.

'Ready?' he asks, though if he thinks I'm going busking in town in a pair of boxers and nowt else he's bonkers. 'Hurry up, man,' he says. 'Deela won't want to see you with no clothes on.'

I'm sure this busking is a rubbish idea, but I go and grab the clothes off me floor and pull them on. I'm about to go downstairs when there's the sound of the front door again – Deela's here. I look down at me T-shirt. Minging. I rip it off and put on a clean one, pick up the fiddle and put it in the battered old case. Half nine in the morning and I'm as ready as I'll ever be.

As we leave the house, I cannet help glancing at the Robsons' place but it isn't likely they'll be up this early. I mean, it's the crack of dawn. Deela's yawning and I just want to crawl back into bed, bad dreams or not. I can hear the Robsons' big ugly dog barking in the back garden.

'I hate that dog,' Deela says. 'It's proper scary.'

Kyle starts to talk about last night, but I shut him down with a look. I'm just grateful they didn't have the dog with them then or no way we'd have got off so easy.

We stand at the bus stop with two old ladies and a man with a kid. The bus is almost empty and we get the front seat up top, which you never get at other times of day. It's good rocking through the streets seeing ordinary people just doing ordinary things. The bus takes a long route past the terraced houses and the local shops to the other end of the park, which stretches like a long thin ribbon of green along the valley. It's pretty much the way we walked home last night. Weird to think of the old mine tunnels below all this. I think about the nightmare, the noise and the heat. Granda used to tell us about the afterdamp – the bad air in the deep tunnels that could suck your breath away. Now he's in the hospital, struggling to breathe. I wonder if he's scared.

We see our first problem with Kyle's plan as soon as we get off the bus. There's no one in town.

'Where is everybody?' Kyle says, looking around.

'We're too early,' Deela says. 'No one else is daft enough to get up this early.'

We walk up and down the main street with all the shops – twice. Partly cos I'm too chicken to just start and partly cos there's no one there to play to.

'We need the right spot,' I keep saying. Kyle rolls his eyes.

Deela goes and gets some pasties from Greggs and we eat them standing by Monument, right in the centre of the town. There's a few people here, hurrying past.

'Should've got a Maccy,' Kyle says, ripping chunks off his pasty and stuffing them in his mouth. 'It's more filling.'

'Eurgh,' Deela says. 'I heard they put bits of horse in them. I wouldn't eat horse, would you? It's just *disgusting*.'

'Conspiracy theory,' I say. 'You're falling down on your research, Deela.'

'Whatever,' Kyle says, licking his fingers and looking round the square. 'Never mind the right place, Archie, we've just got to crack on with this'.

'I like the "we".' I fiddle with me phone – there's a text from Mam. I tell them Granda's definitely being shifted to the other hospital this morning.

'Is he OK?' Deela asks. 'It would be so cool to get him that scooter for when he's out!'

No pressure then.

'I have to be back by this afternoon to go and see him.'

'Better get a move on then,' Deela points at the fiddle case.

Kyle adds, 'This is the best place anyway – loads of people meet here.'

I look around. One man carrying a large box, a woman with a baby in a buggy and two middle-aged women go by. I sigh and lick the grease off me fingers. Make me mind up. What's the worst that can happen? I promise myself I won't care what people think; this is Granda's music and I'm doing it for him.

'Right,' I say and I get the fiddle out. I start out on a silly little bit of a tune, just warming up, like, and then I get going. I shut me eyes and pretend I'm playing it to Granda in our front room and I play through about four songs. Then I stop and open me eyes.

An old woman is standing in front of us with one of them little trolleys old people use. She's got at least three coats on and gloves even though it's summer and as hot again today as yesterday.

'Takes us back,' she says. 'Well done, laddie!' and then she shuffles off and starts rummaging in one of the bins.

'She could've given us fifty p or something,' Kyle says. 'She listened for ages.'

I look at the fiddle case. Empty.

'She's eating out of the bins – she's probably skint,' I say.

'Yeah, someone should help her.' Deela pauses and watches the woman, fascinated. 'But that's minging. It's probably had, like, rats on it, or flies. How can she even *do* that?'

'I s'pose if you're really hungry you'll eat whatever. Can we go home now?' I ask. 'This isn't gonna work, is it? Mebbe we should try the cakes and samosas idea.'

'One more try,' Kyle says. The two of them stand in front of me, looking expectant.

I close me eyes and start to play again.

After a few minutes I cannet resist looking to see if I'm still playing to a bag lady or perhaps nobody at all. Deela's going up to a group of people, talking to them, showing them her phone screen. They give her some money and she goes on to another group.

Suddenly there are quite a few people in the square and more come up out of the Metro station entrance. Some are hanging around waiting to meet up and I have an actual audience, listening. A little kid starts dancing in front of me, the way little kids do – not caring if anyone sees him or laughs at him, just waving his arms and then throwing himself down on the ground like he's been watching street dancers and knows the moves. His mam literally has to tear him away, giving him a coin to stick in me case and a bag of crisps to bribe him to come with her. Kyle's working the crowd as well, grinning like a maniac. I see a lad standing against the entrance to the shopping centre, staring at us. It looks like Tyler Richards, but he's gone so quick it's hard to tell. Mebbe he just looked like him. Small, skinny, shaved hair – bit like Kyle, really. But not as enthusiastic.

'I told you,' Kyle says, grinning as he passes. 'That scooter's as good as bought.'

After a few hours there's about five other buskers competing with us and two have amps, so we call it a day. We've made about eighty quid, which is nowhere near enough but feels amazing. I cannet believe one of Kyle's ideas is finally paying off. Or that I had the guts to play in front of all them people.

We decide to walk home as the bus isn't cheap and we don't want to spend all the money for the scooter on fares. It takes ages. We cut across the city through the student areas, which are dead quiet this time of year. We walk up through the long rows of terraced houses, older than the ones we live in. These have no gardens at the front, just yards that lead on to long, empty, back lanes. We're hot and tired and it feels like I'm lugging a coffin, not a fiddle. The case keeps banging against me legs. We go into the park but from the other side of the valley. It's cool and shady and there's a coffee cart selling drinks and ice creams.

'A few quid won't make much difference,' Kyle says, licking his lips. 'We can go again tomorrow and earn more.'

So we get ice lollies and sit in the shade under the trees.

'This is like . . . this is just the best,' Kyle says. 'Us mates, together, doing something for Granda. Actually making real money!'

I finish me ice lolly and roll over, me hot face against the cool of the ground. I didn't sleep well last night but now I can feel the tension dropping away. There's a drone of bees on the big flower bed and I let myself drift into sleep. Kyle and Deela's voices blend and blur.

Suddenly, the boy from the park is next to us.

'Where's the fiddle, Archie Bell?' he says. 'Hold on tight to it.' There's a banging noise, a sudden shout.

I jolt upright. I look down and see Deela and Kyle've been busy. They've sprinkled me all over with bits of grass and daisies. I feel stupid and start to brush it off, but Deela laughs. 'Could've been worse. Kyle wanted to write on your head, only we didn't have a pen.'

I stare round.

'Did yous see that lad from the park?' I say. 'The one who told us to gan home?'

They both shake their heads like I've lost the plot.

Maybe it's the shock of everything that happened yesterday, these weird dreams that seem so real. Embarrassed, I look at me phone. It's later than I'd realised.

'I better get home,' I say. 'It's visiting hours. I need to see Granda.'

8

It's about four o'clock and me and Mam
are walking up to the hospital in silence.
Mam looks wrecked – dead white and
tired. She's taken time off work to get home
early so we can go to the hospital together.
She's got a bag of clothes and stuff for
Granda.

We cut through the Spinney past the
Not-Library. There's no sign of Gadget Guy,
just a bit of spray paint on the grass marking
where he's scanned the ground. There's a
woman standing at the bus stop but she
doesn't look at us, just stares straight
forward. It's the Robsons' mam. I look round,
checking, but there's no sign of them. I feel

like I'll be looking over me shoulder for the rest of me life.

Mam walks fast for all she's tired. 'That poor woman,' she says when we're further up the hill. 'Had a hard paper round, that one.' She always says that when she means someone's had a tough time. 'Them boys of hers must break her heart.'

I don't say nothing, never mind that they'll probably break me arms first.

'Don't you get involved with them and their silly gangs,' she adds.

I shake me head. A hot surge of panic about what happened last night races through me, but Mam's got too much on her mind for me to worry her with owt else. We pass the Co-op.

'It'll be a lot easier to visit Granda now he's back on this side of the city,' Mam says. 'We can just pop in – no buses, no hanging around. But you don't have to come to the hospital every day,' she adds as we reach the top of the hill. 'He wouldn't expect you to.'

'I want to.'

She smiles and squeezes me hand.

The hospital is proper massive. We go up
in the enormous lift. You could get an
elephant on a trolley in one of them lifts, it's
as if they think there's gonna be a rush on at
visiting time, like at a football match or
summat. I lean on the button. We rise –
slowly, slowly – and then walk along a
corridor with these rubbish pictures of faded
flowers. What's the point of pictures that
make you feel worse than you already feel?
You look at one of them pictures and you
want to lie down and die. I feel sick that
Granda's stuck in here.

He's propped in a bed at the end of a
ward with tubes coming out of his arm.
Another old man is snoring in the corner
with an oxygen mask on. Granda opens his
eyes like he's lifting weights.

'It's me fave . . . me favourite . . . eourgh, eough, eourgh . . . grandson,' he finally manages to choke out.

I smile but me face feels stiff and awkward.

Mam pulls up two chairs and plonks herself down. She starts wittering on, like mams do, telling him she's brought some grapes and that she's changed some shifts so she can visit easier.

'Ooh,' she says. 'Guess what! Our syndicate at work won the lottery!'

There's gotta be a catch cos she doesn't look like a woman who's just become a multimillionaire. I lean forward, ready to get excited as she delivers the punchline.

'Wait for it, I won – drum roll – forty quid!'

Granda laughs his rough, coughing laugh. He's dead pleased to see us, I can tell. He keeps looking at me and then looking away again. I sit as close to the bed as I can.

'Mind,' Mam says, looking my way with a funny smile on her face, 'this is better – hot off the press, brand new. A man came in at lunchtime and ordered the party platters for an event.'

Like, wow. I yawn. Boooring. Granda must think so n'all cos his eyes are closing again. I gaze out of the window at the end of the ward. You can see right out over the park and the city buildings to the moor and far over the river to the hills in the distance. I wonder what it used to look like before all the houses and the big office buildings, when it was woods, farms and little coal mines. Mam goes on.

'He runs a recording studio in the Ouseburn Valley down near the Tyne. He's got a folk band and guess what? He's wanting younger players to do some gigs and recordings, appeal to a new audience, he says.' Her voice is getting loud and excited.

'Mam,' I say, nudging her. 'You'll wake them all up.' But when I look at the old guy in the corner I figure he's half dead and nowt's gonna wake him up. Mam carries on.

73

'He just got talking, not knowing about you being a fiddle player. He said he'd seen a lad in town just this mornin' playing some old songs, got him thinking.'

Me ears are burning. I haven't told her about the scooter plan and no way can I tell her in front of Granda. Not till we're a bit closer to the amount we need.

'He said he was gonna talk to him, but he up and went before he had a chance. But that lad's loss is your gain, cos I said, "My son plays. And he knows loads of old songs passed down in the family with the old fiddle as well".'

Granda's eyes ping open and his breath ratchets up a notch. I realise they're both staring at me.

'It's like it's meant to be, Archie,' she says. 'You'll do it, won't you?' She's pleading. 'You'll go and play for him? Fogg, he's called.'

I look at Granda's eyes, swimming with water. She could've told me this on the walk up, but I realise why she's saved this news till now. She knows I've never liked playing

in front of people and that I would say no.
Only I cannet say no in front of Granda.
Especially not now. If me life depended on it,
I couldn't say no in front of him. It'll be
awkward – even worse than the busking. A
proper professional listening to me. No
getting away with mistakes.

Granda's struggling to sit up, pulling at
the oxygen mask, trying to speak. I look
down, rub me fingers against me jeans.

'OK' I say, not very convincing. I try again.
'Yeah, that would be great!'

Mam's easy fooled. Granda gives me a
searching look, but he relaxes back on to the
pillow. I put me hand out and our fingers
touch. He doesn't speak, just moves one
finger very slowly against mine. I explore the
grooves and ridges of his fingers with me
thumb, remembering when his hands moved
so fast on the strings. *It should be you*, I
think. *It should be you, recording. Not me. I'm
rubbish compared to you.*

Life isn't fair. But I don't say anything
at all.

9

It's hot all night and I twist and turn, me
thoughts tumbling around like rats in a bag.
I hardly sleep until it's light. I figure we don't
need to get up so early now we know there's
no point going busking till after ten, but
same as yesterday Kyle's banging on me
door well before I'm ready.

We check it's safe to leave the house.
Their curtains are drawn – no sign of the
Robsons – so we slink down the alley and
into the trees of the Spinney. Deela catches
us up, hurrying across the grass. She's got
sunglasses and a purple T-shirt on over black
jeans and suddenly looks more grown up.
Must be the glasses. Her hair is shining in
the sunlight – a long straight ponytail today.

Gadget Guy's back, prodding the ground with his survey machine over near the Not-Library. He's got a girl with him, like he's brought reinforcements. She's tall, sipping a take-away coffee and looking like a model from a photo shoot who's got lost.

'Hi there!' He still sounds dead posh but less angry than the last time I saw him. 'Thank you so much, Adila, for looking after me the other day. I think I was more upset than I realised. I must come round and thank your mum for the tea and samosas, they were fantastic.'

Deela smiles at him. 'That's OK,' she says. She told us yesterday she thought he was just her big sister's type – posh, rich and demanding. But the way she's grinning at him I think mebbe he's her type, too – even if he looks way too old for her.

'Did you get your rucksack back?' Kyle says.

'No, the police are useless. But now Tasha's here it's a bit easier to keep an eye on things. And she's got a car, so we can lock stuff away.' He glances towards the closed-up library building and I see a shiny white Mini parked right outside it.

'Oh, that's a really cute car,' Deela says. 'My sister would kill for one of them.'

Tasha grins. 'It was a twenty-first birthday present,' she says.

Deela's eyebrows rocket off her forehead. Her dad's a taxi driver and she really knows cars. She knows how much they cost, n'all.

'I should never have got started by myself,' Gadget Guy says. 'But I was told this wasn't a bad area.'

'It's *not* a bad area,' I say, annoyed.

Tasha sips her coffee uncomfortably.

'Most people are just ordinary,' Deela says, 'like my mam and dad, working hard, bringing up their kids. It's always been dead safe here.'

I shoot her a quick grin.

'Well,' Kyle adds, 'it was till them lads moved in.'

78

'Better get going.' I hoist the fiddle case up on me shoulder, but Deela doesn't take the hint.

'Anyway, what are you scanning for?' She points at the machine.

'I'm doing a whole site preliminary survey,' Gadget Guy says. 'It's part of a bigger project where we try to map what used to be on the ground at various sites across the region and match it up with the old maps of underground workings. Here, no one recorded the surface buildings before they knocked them down to build your estate. That's what I'm trying to plot.'

Tasha nods. 'The mines round here are really interesting. This city has, like, a ghost city below ground.'

A ghost city. I picture all the tunnels Granda told us about but with people still living and working away down there. I know she doesn't mean that, but for a moment the image is clear in my mind.

'D'you get paid?' Kyle asks.

'Well, no, but it'll count for my degree,' Gadget Guy says. 'And Tash is just a lovely person who's helping me out.'

'Yeah, though you owe me for it.' She laughs and drinks some more coffee.

'What's the point, then?' Kyle asks. 'Who cares? We know the story. There's a board by the bus stop you can read. And history's not gonna change, is it?'

Tasha smiles. 'But what people *think* they know and what actually happened in the past – can be different.'

Gadget Guy laughs. 'Yeah, I bet you don't know that this isn't even the mine where all the men died? So that information board's wrong.'

'No way,' Kyle says. 'We live here and we all know this is it! The miners got trapped and died right under here and the trees got planted in their memory. You cannet change the past, man.'

Gadget Guy pushes his hands through his thick curly hair. 'No, this mine came later.

The one that flooded was much closer to the river where the parks are now. Stories get garbled or lost, things get forgotten. Don't you think understanding what really happened matters?'

I'm gobsmacked that what we all know may not be true, but Kyle narrows his eyes and I can tell he doesn't believe them.

'So,' Deela says, 'it's not the past that changes, just what we know about it?'

Gadget Guy nods. 'Well put.'

Kyle gives a sniff and pushes his hand over his head, smoothing down the hair he hasn't got. 'Well, I'm not bothered where they died,' he says, adding in some effin's that we all ignore. 'It's the future I'm interested in – and the future says we're gannin to town. We have plans, right, Archie? Deela?'

He struts off and we watch him head to the bus stop.

'Don't mind him,' Deela says. 'I think it's dead interesting. Almost like you're a CSI or a detective but for the past. Bye Josh, bye Tasha.'

We follow Kyle to the bus stop.

'Really. Look at Kyle doing his swagger – it doesn't fool no one.'

'Josh?' I say.

'Well, you didn't think he was really called Gadget Guy, did you?' she says, adjusting her sunglasses.

10

The bus is pulling into the stop when Tyler Richards shoots past on his bike. He stares hard at us. I hold tight to the fiddle and climb on.

Deela shrugs. 'If he wasn't so annoying I'd be impressed he's up this early.'

When we get to town we go straight to Monument this time. No messing around. I still feel sick with nerves, but knowing I survived yesterday and that people seemed to like it – at least, no one threw anything at me – makes me feel like I can do it again. Kyle and Deela stand with me while I set up me case and get the fiddle out. I close me eyes and start to play.

I've been playing a good hour or more, with Kyle and Deela going round the square talking to people and telling them what we're raising cash for, when a man comes over.

'D'you have a performance permit?' he asks.

'A what?'

'A performance permit.'

'Aye, definitely!' Kyle springs up behind us out of nowhere. The man looks at us hard and grins. 'I won't tell on you, mate – I've busked myself – but you've gotta watch out for them inspectors. They come round and if you haven't got a permit, they'll fine you.' He drops a coin in me case and walks away.

'Great,' I say.

Kyle pushes his hand over his head. 'What's a man got to do round here to make a bit of cash? Why's everything so stitched up?'

'And how will we know when we see an inspector? What does one even look like?' I add.

'Don't suppose they go around wearing a hat with "Busking Inspector" on it.'

Deela comes over, having seen that I've stopped playing.

'What's the matter?'

I explain.

'I know!' she says. 'Let's make sure there's not much money in the case so if they catch you and it looks like you've not made anything, then they might just let you off with a warning.'

'Worth a try,' Kyle says. 'That bloke could be lying. Mebbe he wants the pitch for himself.' He scoops most of the money out of the case and puts it into his pocket. 'Sounding good though. Weird how them old songs make you, like, feel stuff.'

After another half hour I'd really like to stop and get a drink and summat to eat. I'm on edge as well, looking out for anyone who might be an inspector. As me eyes scan the square I can see Deela, but have no idea where Kyle's got to. There's a tall lad with red hair coming round the corner, then another. Me heart stops.

Robsons.

I cannet believe it – I've never seen them out this early! I keep playing but I feel sick. Can it be a coincidence? I remember thinking I saw Tyler Richards yesterday and that he saw us getting the bus this morning. He must've told them I was making a fool of myself, trying to make money. And they'd be interested in both.

Me stomach's churning but me hands stay steady. One twin points at me, holds his fingers to his head – *POW* – like he's shooting a gun, then laughs. I try to ignore him. They wouldn't try owt in front of so many people, would they? And this is the city centre! There are CCTV cameras everywhere. If anywhere's safe it must be here. I carry on playing, but I keep me eyes open now, just in case. After a few minutes they disappear into the crowd, so perhaps it *is* a coincidence. I relax a bit and start on another tune – one of Granda's favourites. I picture him in the hospital bed and say a wish or a kind of prayer.

'Hang on, Granda,' I whisper.

Deela bounces up looking pleased with herself.

'Doing well,' she says. 'I've been showing everyone Granda's picture and saying how bad he needs the scooter.' She waves her phone at me. 'Most people give something.'

I watch a little kid put a coin in the old case.

'How much longer?' I ask. Me and Kyle still haven't told her about how the Robsons chased us last night, but seeing them has put me on edge.

'Till we've got as much as yesterday!' she says. 'We've made about thirty quid already.'

'Big money!' Robson One is suddenly there, leaning in over Deela's shoulder.

I dunno where he even came from – it's like he's come out of the ground, a zombie from a grave or a bad stink coming up out of a sewer. I look around for the other one.

'What's it worth? That old fiddle?' He puts his hand out like he's going to grab it, laughing. The laugh has an echo as Robson Two finally appears.

I stop playing and just stand there, clutching the fiddle to me chest. I remember the voice I heard in the park, *'Hold on tight to the fiddle!'* If owt happens to it, it'll kill Granda – break his heart. Robson One gives a sharp-toothed grin.

'Careful now,' he says, dead low. 'We wouldn't want to, like, smash that old fiddle, would we? Looks like it might just, you kna, fall to bits.' He slaps me on the back like he's me mate, only it's so hard I nearly fall over. Under his breath he says, 'What's the matter, fiddle kid? Not gonna give us your stand-up routine again? You're *dead* funny, you are.'

Deela shoots me a look, as if to say, *What?!*

'*Dead* funny,' Robson Two echoes, like I've not got the joke.

I stare around frantically. I wonder if I start shouting, will someone help.

People keep passing without even looking at us. Do they think we're just a gang of kids messing on, having a laugh? Only it's not funny. And where the hell is Kyle? Some bodyguard he is. But then me gut lurches. Mebbe they've already got him and he's slumped unconscious in an alley. Robson One leans right on to Deela, like, way too close and goes to put his arm round her. She flinches and tries to pull away. A woman gives us a look as she passes like she's concerned, but she doesn't stop. Deela, normally so quick to speak up, just stands there.

'Leave her alone,' I say, but me voice comes out all weedy with a quiver in it. He laughs.

'And you're gonna stop us, fiddle kid? What you gonna do, beat us to death with your little stick thing?'

'It's a bow,' Deela says, her voice coming back, trying to jerk away from his arm. 'Get your hands off me.' She twists away from him. 'I'm not scared of you!' But her voice is high, so I know she is.

'Feisty. I like that in a lass. Had me eye on you for a while now. You dinnet have to hang with these losers, you kna.' He nods at Robson Two. 'You owe us, fiddle boy.'

Robson Two strolls towards me, slow and easy. He leans forward, looking like he's gonna put a coin in me fiddle case. Only he scoops up the money – every single bit.

'You need some protection,' he says. 'Kids like you cannet look after themselves, can they?' He steps back, sliding it into his pocket. 'There's sharks out there, you kna.'

'Give it back!' Deela says. 'That's Granda's money! And there's cameras all round here – you're gonna get caught. You'll end up in prison like your dad.'

Robson One grabs her arm again. 'Only if you tell on us.' He puts his hand under her chin and forces her face up to look at him. 'And you won't. D'you kna why?'

Her body is rigid as he pulls her close and whispers in her ear. I see her shiver and close her eyes. It feels like a long moment before he lets her go.

'And if *you* tell,' he pokes me in the chest, 'it's her'll pay for it. That goes for the other little grass n'all. See ya, losers!'

Robson Two giggles. 'Aye, when yous least expect it,' he adds.

They stroll off into the crowd with all our cash.

We don't shout 'thief!' We don't chase them through the streets. Nobody notices them. Nobody jumps out and arrests them. I clutch me fiddle and watch them disappear. And the dream of Granda driving down the park on his own scooter, smiling at the birds and the trees – that disappears, too.

11

I stuff the fiddle into the empty case and turn to Deela.

'You OK? What did he say to you?'

Of course she's not OK – stupid question. Deela doesn't scare easily but she's shaking. I want to hit summat. Or someone.

Her eyes are wide and scared, and I can hardly hear what she says, her voice is that quiet. Even her lips are barely moving, like bad animation.

'It doesn't matter. They didn't mean it. They were just trying to be hard.'

'They're wrecking everything. We're, like, their dream victims. What did he say to you?'

She shakes her head. 'He said . . .' She looks away. She's fiddling with the edge of her T-shirt, not looking at me. 'Anyway, he was just trying to scare me. I'm not scared. D'you think it's gone cold?' The city is sweltering in the sun but she's shivering. I want to give her a hug, only I dunno if she'd want me to.

'Kyle!' I burst out. 'Where was he when we needed him? Where the hell is he now?'

'Get real, Archie,' she says, rubbing her arms like she's frozen. 'What could Kyle have done? He's even smaller than you are. He talks tough but no way is he hard – why d'you think he hangs round with you and me?' She keeps playing with the hem of her T-shirt, like if she can just smooth it out, everything'll be OK.

'They're just scum, that's what,' I say. 'Howay, let's gan home. This thing's over, right?'

She's still shaking but she follows me. I don't even care about the money any more; I just feel sick like our whole lives are gonna be dogged by them lads forever and it's me and Kyle's fault that Deela's got sucked into it. We're well on their radar now and nowt we do will change it. The way he grabbed Deela like he was gonna force a kiss on her, like he could do whatever he wanted, makes me feel so . . .

I kick out at an empty can and it bounces off the wall of the shopping centre. An old woman gives me a look so I kick it again, hard. It doesn't help me feel better. Deela doesn't even notice, just walks away.

We go the opposite way to the twins, past the shops. Suddenly Kyle appears like a small blond rabbit out of a magician's hat looking absolutely fine.

'Where the hell where you when we needed you? The Robson lads crashed us. They took all the cash and then, Deela . . .' I dry up. It's not the time. She's gazing off into space, her eyes bugging out of her head and her mouth doing a weird upside-down smile. She doesn't say anything, just keeps walking – fast. We follow her but she passes the bus stop and seems set on walking all the way home, which is a hell of a way.

'I saw,' Kyle says, trotting behind us. 'I figured we had to save some of the cash. I hid in a shop, but I was watching the whole time.'

'Thanks for that,' I say sarcastically. 'Really good of you to keep an eye on us, cheers, mate.'

'I knew they'd take it all, man. I kna how lads like them think.'

'Whatever.' He's trying to make out what he did was clever when I know he was just being a coward.

'Look, I think we've got about thirty quid here and I didn't want them to nick it off us. At least we've not lost everything.'

Deela's really shifting and is way ahead of us.

'What's up with her?' Mr Sensitive, Kyle.

'She's upset.' I want to shake him, to stop talking about this and catch up with her. I start to jog.

'I bet she was dead scared – I know I was crapping myself when I saw him put his arm round her like a . . .' Kyle is panting along next to me, 'a python or summat. A monster big snake gonna swallow her. There was this story in the news—'

'So why ask if you know? It's not like you helped.' I run harder. The fiddle case keeps bumping against me leg. Kyle's dropping behind. 'You are so unfit,' I say.

He gives me a look and stops running. Great. Deela's in trauma, we've lost half the cash and me and Kyle are about to actually row for the second time in two days – and it's all them boys' fault. The whole day is just wrecked. The whole summer is wrecked. Our whole lives are—

Me phone beeps. I stop and check it.

'Mam's going up the hospital this afternoon.'

Kyle starts to walk again. 'Don't tell Granda, will you? About the scooter,' he says. 'It's gotta be a surprise. Or mebbe when we're a bit closer to the total you could tell him then. It might give him summat to get better for, to aim for, you know.'

'You don't get it, do you? It's over. It was a daft idea. Deela'll probably never come into town with us again, and I'm not looking stupid so I can put money into them lads' pockets. Even if we came every day and didn't get done by an inspector – or ripped off by them Robsons – it'll still take forever to earn enough.' I hitch the fiddle up higher. 'I'd be better selling the stupid fiddle than playing it.'

But that's not true. Not even if it was worth a million pounds, which it sure as hell isn't. Pictures flash through me head of the night Dad left. He said he could get a hundred quid for it and Granda went radge.

'Get out! Stay out! You're no son of mine!' His voice was so loud for a man who never shouted – it made the walls shake. He'd pointed at the door and I wanted to laugh cos it was like out of a movie, only it was Granda and Dad and it was real.

'That's our history, our blood in that fiddle and you'd sell it for a mess of pottage?' Granda had shouted. Dad went through the door and it slammed behind him. What the hell was pottage? I never dared ask. And Dad never came back.

Deela suddenly sits down on the kerb and me and Kyle finally manage to catch up. We're out of the centre of town now and there aren't so many shops or people, just cars swishing by quiet houses. The bus whooshes past. I sigh. We could've been home in minutes – now it'll take ages.

'You cryin', Deela?' Kyle crouches down next to her. I stand awkwardly.

A woman passes and looks at us then looks away, not sure if she should get involved. She walks on a bit, hesitates, turns and calls from a distance like we're dangerous animals.

'Are you alright?'

Deela lifts her head, her eyes wet. She nods.

Kyle puts his arms round her and gives her a hug. I should've done that. Why couldn't I do that?

'She's just a bit upset,' he says. Stating the obvious as usual. 'But we're her mates, we'll look after her.'

Deela hugs him back then pulls away and nods again. The woman smiles and walks on – relieved, I bet. People don't want to be sucked into trouble.

I wait. After a while sitting on the kerb Deela scrubs at her eyes and says, 'OK, right. I'm OK. I just . . . I guess I just . . .' and then she starts to cry again.

'Her dad's gonna totally kill us,' Kyle whispers to me.

He probably *will* kill us, but only if she tells him what happened. And only if the Robsons don't get us first.

'I'm sorry,' she says finally. 'I'm not sad.' She sniffs and rummages in her jeans pocket for a tissue. 'I just hate how he made me feel so frightened. I don't want to live scared!'

Once Deela gets up we power on till we reach the bridge over the Dene – nearly home now, though home doesn't feel safe any more. She stops and rests her head against the metal railing, gazing out over the trees. This is becoming like a habit, stopping here.

'How are we gonna get them off our backs?' I say. We all know who I'm talking about.

'What's their problem? We've not done *anything* to them,' Deela says. 'They're just thugs. They gave me a fright in town but no way are they going to get away with going after us, day after day.' She stands up straight, her eyes narrowing.

'Well,' Kyle says. 'I guess it depends on, you kna, your standpoint. I mean, helping Gadget Guy grass them up to the police – naebody likes a grass, right?' He looks down at his feet.

'So,' Deela gives him a hard, red-eyed stare. 'You telling me it's yous and my fault, for helping a victim of crime?' She gives a lot of emphasis to 'victim'.

I sigh. 'Haway, we need a solution, not a philosophical debate!' but Kyle is shaking his head, like a rabbit caught in headlights.

'No, no way, Deela! Anyways,' he grins. 'It was Archie got them proper roused up, making fun of them in the park last night.'

Deela looks at us both. 'Have I missed something?'

I grab Kyle and get him in a headlock, cos I really want him to stop talking. He starts yelling so I let go. Deela's rolling her eyes, which are kind of puffy from crying. I've never seen her cry like that.

'Sorry,' I say. 'You're right. We've both messed up. But it's not fair they're picking on you. We all really need to keep out of their way, let it settle.'

She shakes her head. 'No. That's pathetic, Archie, you know we cannet hide from them

101

forever. If we tell the police about that iPad we saw them with, when they search their house—'

'By the time the police go round Gadget Guy's stuff won't be there,' I interrupt. 'Even the Robsons aren't stupid enough to keep hold of stolen stuff. They probably use kids like Tyler Richards to look after it. And if they find we've done owt else to get at them they'll kill us. Literally kill us.'

She gives me a stern look. I'm glad she's stopped crying, but this new avenging Deela is proper scary. She shakes her head, determined.

'I'm going home now,' she says, her voice wobbling a bit. Then her chin goes up and she looks like you really don't want to mess with her. 'I'm gonna get them off our estate if it's the last thing I do.'

Trouble is, it probably will be.

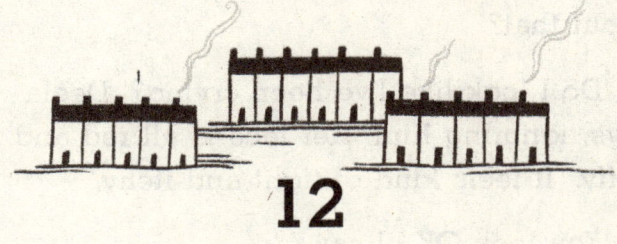

12

Normally we'd split at the alley and go in different directions home but Deela starts to walk slower and slower. She'll have to walk right past the Robsons' house and it's taken us so long to walk back they could be there already. I'm sick to me stomach – I can't begin to think how she feels.

'Deela,' I say. 'Mam's still at work for a bit and I kind of don't want to go back to the empty house without Granda there. Can I come round yours till it's time to meet her at the hospital?'

'Oh, yeah! Has your mam got any of them samosas left, Deela?' Kyle says, assuming that if I'm going he is n'all. 'They're better than any you can buy. She could set up a business selling them. Has she thought about that?'

'Do I look like I've been crying?' Deela says, ignoring him. Her face is all red and puffy. 'It feels kind of tight and itchy.'

'You look OK,' I say.

'Like hell you do!' Kyle says. Mr Sensitive strikes again. I thump him on the arm, but he just shrugs.

'It's not like I care,' she says. 'But if I look like I've been crying Mam'll notice. She'll want to know everything and, well, I don't want to talk about it yet. I really don't want Mam and Dad getting all worked up – I'm too tired for drama. I can't believe I let them Robsons rule me, that I didn't kick and scream or call for help. There were loads of people and we just took it. *I* just took it.'

'What were you meant to do?' I ask. 'D'you really think people would've chased them off if you called for help? They probably thought he was our mate just messing on.'

'So, what did he say that scared you?' Kyle says.

'You can tell us,' I add.

Deela screws up her face. 'He just said he could find me any time. And he'd hurt me bad. I was looking straight in his eyes and they were, like . . . empty.' Her voice fades for a moment. 'But mebbe it was just talk to frighten me.'

'Well it sure frightens me,' I say. 'You can be brave but you can also be dead. It's better to just leave it. Let them have the money. Nothing's worth your life. Granda always says a really brave person can walk away cos they don't need to show off.'

'Maybe I should get a knife,' Kyle says. 'Just so's we can protect ourselves. Then we'd know we were, like, ready for them.'

Deela stops dead. 'Are you off your head?'

Kyle looks at her. 'Well I know it's not, like, right and that, but I'd only use it to defend us.'

'Remember that assembly we had? Tell him, Archie, you were there.'

I shrug. 'Yeah, and so were you, Kyle. That guy with the man bun?'

Deela says, 'Prison! Just for carrying one!' She gives a dramatic pause. 'And loads of kids get stabbed by their own knife anyway!'

Kyle rolls his eyes. 'It was dead boring, that talk. I wasn't really listening.'

'Really?' she says. 'Nobody would ever know.'

Kyle's ears go pink and I grin. It's good to have the bossy Deela back, telling us off.

The Spinney wood is empty – no kids playing out, no dogwalkers, no Gadget Guy. Mebbe it's because it's so hot. I cannet remember a time when the city felt like this. I send Kyle through the alley first to make up for abandoning us. When he waves the all-clear, we run out and speed past the Robsons' house.

'We can't live like this!' Deela says as we barrel through her front door. We stand in the hallway. Bad luck for us her big sister, Nabila, is coming down the stairs.

'Deela? What's happened to you? You look terrible!'

'Thanks for nothing.' Deela always says Nabila has eagle eyes and sniffs out trouble.

'You're all, like, puffy round your eyes. You been crying? You need a cucumber face mask.' She tips her head back and stares at me and Kyle. 'What've you done to her? Deela, you shouldn't hang out with boys all the time. You're too old for that now. You should have proper girl friends.'

Awkward. Me and Kyle stand there, sweating. I kind of push the fiddle behind my legs.

'They haven't done anything,' Deela says. 'And last time I hung out with a group of girls they treated me like dirt. Archie and Kyle are like cousins.'

'Oh, so they cut off your hair and throw you in the swimming pool, right?'

Deela laughs. 'She's just bitter – that's what our cousins did to *her* when she was younger.'

Nabila grins. 'OK, but seriously, what's happened?' She puts her arm round Deela. 'You know you can tell me. I'm here for you, little sis.'

'I'm just really hot,' Deela lies. 'I feel like I can't even breathe. You go through to the kitchen,' she says to us. 'Tell Mam I'm just going up to have a shower and get changed – it's too hot for black jeans.' She rushes off up the stairs.

'Hurry back!' Nabila calls. 'Mam said she needs help cooking this afternoon – she has loads to do for the party next week!' Nabila turns back and looks at us.

'At least she's home safe,' Kyle says.

Nabila narrows her eyes. 'Why wouldn't she be?'

'One of them Robson twins give her a fright,' he blurts out.

'Kyle!' I elbow him in the ribs and give him a death stare.

Nabila rolls her eyes. 'I *knew* something had happened!'

'It's nowt,' I say. There's a long beat of silence and I can feel me face going red. 'It's no big deal.' I feel mean saying it was nothing, but Deela did say she didn't want to tell them. Unfortunately, Nabila's not stupid.

She opens her mouth to do the full-on interrogation but their mam shouts from the kitchen.

'Nabila, you going to let them stand out in the hall all the day?'

Nabila opens the door and Kyle goes past her. She looks at us.

'No biggie. I'll find out, you know.'

I step in, wishing we'd left Deela at her front door.

*

It's like a restaurant inside the kitchen, the big table covered in samosas – some cooked, some still waiting to be fried – and little bowls of different spices and neatly chopped vegetables. Their mam's standing there working.

Kyle sniffs. 'That smells deeee-vine, Mrs A,' he says. He's always called Mrs Akthar that and she doesn't seem to mind. 'Those onion bhajis?'

'Pakoras. Do you want to try them, Kyle, Archie? Boys are always hungry. Nabila, help get plates while I fry the next batch.'

Before we got friends with Deela, I didn't even know you could make them at home, I thought you could only get them at the Co-op in plastic packets.

Kyle sits down at the table and gives a deep, happy sigh.

'Have you thought of going into business, Mrs A?'

Nabila laughs. 'She sort of is,' she says. 'Only they don't pay her proper! Every auntie and uncle we have wants her to cook for weddings and birthday parties. Most of this'll go in the freezer for the big event next weekend.'

'I like doing it,' Mrs Akthar says, gently sliding the pakoras into a large pan of oil so hot it's smoking. 'Nabila, open the back door, get some air! And anyway, they do cover my costs.'

'You should make a profit,' Kyle says. 'A big fat profit.' He bites into a freshly cooked samosa. 'Mmm. I swear these are the best thing I've ever tasted.'

'Archie, how is your grandfather today?' she asks.

I kind of nod and mumble 'OK.'

I can hear the shower going upstairs. It just keeps going and going, like Deela's never gonna come out of it.

Deela's mam prefers us to hang out at their house rather than at mine with just me and Granda. Her parents are protective – but in a good way. They worry about everything.

When we come round her mam always feeds us and seems pleased to see us, but I've never felt so awkward here as I do now. Like I've let them down.

Mr Akthar comes in for his lunch and the awkwardness is multiplied.

'I've no bookings for half an hour – just enough time for something tasty,' he says, washing his hands at the sink. He glances at us but doesn't say hello. Deela's mam puts the kettle on and Nabila gets another plate and loads it with food for him. As he eats, he starts going on about the state of the roads.

'So many potholes, it's crazy like Wild West out there. Some big enough to hide a fridge in – they'll wreck the suspension! It's not cheap you know, to replace suspension in cars.'

I'm on the edge of my chair, ready to leave, but Kyle is nodding, making agreeing noises and stuffing his face.

'Cheers Mrs A, much appreciated,' he says as she hands him a cup of tea. I want to scream.

112

Then Mr Akthar moves on to moaning about the street. 'It's like a junkyard along our street, lowering the neighbourhood. Like turning it into a slum, right? These new people don't look after their garden. I think they're druggies.'

Nabila says, 'Yeah and they've give our Deela a proper fright today!'

There's a gasp from the doorway. Deela is standing there, hands on hips.

'Nabila! Shut up! Why you always interfering?' She gives me and Kyle a look that says she'll lay into us later.

Their mam stands holding the teapot, staring at us all as calm turns to chaos in a moment.

Mr Akthar goes up like a rocket. 'What is this? I told you when they moved in to keep away from those boys! Tell me, was this in the street? What did they do?'

'One of them just . . . said something, that's all. Just words.' Deela rubs her eyes, looking away from her dad. 'I don't want you to, like, overreact—'

'Adila! You tell me every single thing. EVERY THING!'

Kyle says, 'We were only busking in town. You couldn't be safer than at Monument, could you? We're, like, raising money for a scooter for Granda cos he cannet walk now or nothing.'

Have you ever tried to explain something that at the time seemed dead reasonable, but the more you try, the crazier it sounds? Everyone knows Granda and respects him. I see Kyle's hopeful face, like if only he can sell this idea everything will be just fine again.

'It wasn't a bad thing,' Deela says, 'to try and help an old man.'

Mrs Akthar rubs her face with her hands, leaving a smudge of gram flour on her nose. She doesn't say anything, but she doesn't need to as Mr Akthar says plenty. He pulls the story from Deela, bit by bit, until finally he can pin it down.

'Did they touch you? Hurt you?'

There's a long pause.

'No,' Deela says eventually, but she doesn't sound very convincing. I remember the way Robson One put his arm round her and grabbed her chin and tilted her head so she had to stare into his face. 'Sort of,' she says quietly.

Mr Akthar explodes. 'Trouble! Your mother, she says you're young and you need to be free, but this is what happens – throats cut and left in a ditch girls!'

I get up to leave, but Mr Akthar keeps ranting and he's blocking the doorway.

'No more hanging around the streets with boys doing who-knows-what bosking!' he shouts. 'You're grounded, Adila! For the rest of summer vacation. Stay home. Help your mother in the house.'

'Why's it *my* fault?' Deela says. 'Just because I'm a girl. I haven't done anything!'

'Don't answer back! I must get back to work.' Mr Akthar turns and leaves the kitchen. We hear him stamping off down the hall.

Deela's mam is rubbing her eyes with a tea towel. 'How could you let me down, Adila? I tell him all the time, in this country you have the right to choose your own friends. I know you're good boys, Archie and Kyle, but asking people for money in town! It's not how we do things.' She chokes up again, scrunching the tea towel up in her hands.

'We weren't doing anything bad,' Deela says. 'It's the Robsons who are in the wrong here. How's that got forgotten?'

Nabila's leaning against the kitchen worktop. 'Deela, if you'd not been there they couldn't have threatened you.'

'Shut up – you're a sneak!' Deela says.

'Erm, we'll go,' I say, grabbing Kyle by the arm.

'Well, thanks, Mrs A,' he says, finishing off his last samosa.

She picks up a large pan of food and then puts it down again, as if she's forgotten what she needs to do next.

'We can't let people like them win,' Deela says. 'I'm over it. I'm not scared at all.'

Nabila's eyes are wide. 'No way, sis – these are scary people. You ought to be scared of them.'

'Well, I don't want to live life like that.'

'OK, but what if they hurt Dad? There's two of them and only one of him.'

'If he goes round the Robsons and they beat him up, then it'll be *your* fault for telling him.'

'Bye then,' I say and pull Kyle into the hall. As the door closes behind us we hear Deela's mam, her voice raised for the first time ever.

'Adila! *Enough! Go to your room!*'

It's dark, hot. I scratch at me chest, tryin' to pull me skin off, itching with the dirt. I cannet breathe, man, I cannet . . . me lungs fillin' and me legs so heavy I cannet run.

Voices. 'Hauld on, man, I'm comin' for you. Can you not hear the picks? They're comin', they'll get us out. Hauld on.'

'Rob!' I try to shout into the dark but all that comes out is a whisper. I've lost me boy, I've lost him. I reach for his hand, but there's nothing, no one. Just the cold watter lapping me body and me own chokin', whispery voice in the dark.

13

After me and Mam get back from seeing
Granda, she sticks some pasties in the oven
for tea. I move from room to room feeling
like I cannet settle to anything. The air feels
hot and sticky and there's this quiet that's
almost heavy on me chest. I switch on the
telly and leave it playing, but it isn't the
same without Granda watching and
grumbling, laying into all the programmes.

I go to me room and get the fiddle out
again. I stroke the wood. Each dint and bash
must tell a story about some moment, gone. I
think of all the people who've held and
played this fiddle, all the hands – Granda's
last of all.

I start to play. Sad old songs like *Four Pence a Day* and *The Watter of Tyne*. I remember Dad shouting at Granda, 'We divvent need the past round here, what we need is a future.' Seems like I lost Dad and got Kyle to replace him.

After a while Mam comes in and stands against the door. Not much space in my little room.

'We'll see him again tomorrow.' She puts her hand on me shoulder. 'I'm sorry, son, I'd hoped he'd be picking up.' Her voice is flat, tired. 'His lungs are fillin' with fluid. He's drownin' in his own body.' She pauses. 'It's all them years working down the pits. It wrecks you, all that coal dust. Archie, can you ring your dad? He needs to come and see him.'

'No!' I say, putting down the fiddle. 'Granda'll get better, you'll see.'

'You need to give your dad a chance to see him.'

'But Granda won't want to! He told him to go. He said he was a waster and he never wanted to see him again!'

She just stands there looking at me. 'Your Granda's never stopped loving him, even though he's a waste of space . . .' She stops. 'I'd want to see you, whatever happened.'

But honestly, I dunno where Dad is. The last time I tried his number it just wasn't working – like he'd disappeared off the face of the earth. I've lied to her before but it's harder now with the way she keeps looking at me . . .

'I dunno where he is.'

'But he rang you on your birthday, you said?'

'I lied. He's changed his phone. I dunno where he is any more than you do.'

Mam puts her hands to her face. She doesn't say owt, just stands there breathing. Hell, you'd think she wanted Dad to come back. Dunno what she thinks he's gonna do to help, like. She turns away, but as she goes

121

through the door, she pauses. Her voice is dead quiet and sort of questioning. 'You'll go and see that bloke, Fogg, about the music, won't you? For your Granda – it'll make him so proud. Fogg says there might be some money in it as well.'

I nod. 'If you *really* want me to.' But it comes out sounding like a stroppy kid. I wish I could be nicer to her.

'He said he could see you tomorrow, remember? I've got the address written down.' She sounds so tired, defeated. 'You won't forget, will you, Archie?' She turns to go. 'Don't be long comin' down, them pasties should be ready now.' She closes the door quietly behind her and I draw my bow across the strings, listening to each note as it hangs in the air. I play them again and again until each sound is as pure and clean and itself as it can be.

Saddo boy, fiddling on. I put the fiddle down and message Kyle about going down the Ouseburn to play for the old guy tomorrow, ask him to come with me. Thinking about playing for a stranger makes me feel sick. He doesn't get back to me. So I guess I'm gannin on me own then.

*

We're just eating tea when there's banging on the door. It's Deela's dad in a right radge. When I open it, he marches straight in.

'I have come to see your mother.'

Mam comes out into the hall and stops dead.

'Your boy, he has taken my Adila to the town and got her involved in trouble!'

'You what? What's this, Archie?' She's holding a half-eaten pasty in one hand. He looks at it and sniffs. I think they smell pretty good but he looks seriously not impressed. 'Mr Akthar?' she says, surprised.

'He took her begging for money. Put her at risk.'

Mam just keeps staring like her eyes will pop out.

'You did what, Archie? Why were you begging? What's happened to Adila? I'm sorry, Mr Akthar, come into the kitchen. I'll put the kettle on.' She goes through so we both have to follow.

'We were busking,' I tell her as she fills the kettle.

Mr Akthar looks less radgy sitting down.

'Some lads took our money,' I continue, trying to keep it simple for her. 'Deela got scared.'

'Did you know them?' Mam asks, getting to the nub of it too quickly.

I look away and shrug. I don't want her to have anything else to worry about.

Mr Akthar wags a finger at me. 'You know full well. Those boys opposite! But whatever fights between you boys, my Adila will not be dragged into it. Boys in gang stuff!' He snorts.

I want to say, 'You're at the wrong house, mate. Go and get the lads that did it!' But what if that kicks off a whole load of trouble?

They wouldn't think twice about wrecking his car – or worse.

It's like he can read me mind.

'I will sort those boys!' he says. 'I have been to their house! Adila will stay at home from now on and be safe. Your mother should know you are begging in town, getting in trouble.'

The kettle boils, but Mam just stands there with the teabags in her hand. 'Why were you begging?' she asks again. It's like she's latching on to stray words and can't quite get the whole thing at once.

'*Busking*, not begging,' I say, going red.

Mr Akthar stands up. 'No. No, thank you, no tea. We are done here. Don't you try to see her, right? You keep away from her.'

I nod, dumb. He turns and looks at Mam.

'I know it's not your fault,' he says. 'A boy needs a father.' Then he marches down the hall, out of the door and stamps down the path. He climbs into his cab and drives off, even though he only lives six houses away.

'Well,' Mam says, breathing out in a big whoosh. 'Needs a father! Men are such scumbags. And that's hard on Adila, like she's under house arrest or something.'

'We never made her come – she wanted to! It was Kyle's stupid idea and Deela thought it was a good stupid idea. Them Robsons came after *us*.'

'Didn't I say they're trouble? To keep away from them?'

'It's not like we did owt! They hated us anyway, even before they knew Kyle and Deela helped Gadget Guy when they nicked his rucksack. We think they had his iPad down in the park.' I don't mention them overhearing me and Kyle making fun of them, or them chasing us.

Mam's eyes sort of glaze over. 'Do we live on the same planet? Who on earth is Gadget Guy?'

'It doesn't matter. It's not that I wouldn't have told you, Mam. I just didn't want to worry you. Not on top of everything else.'

She puts her hands up and scrubs them through her short hair until she looks like a bog brush.

'Aye, it is a lot. Can you just try and keep your head down, though, eh?' she pauses. 'Did they actually hurt Adila?'

'No,' I lie. I know you don't need to leave a bruise to hurt someone.

Mam rubs me shoulder. She looks exhausted. 'How much money did they take off you?'

'About thirty quid.'

Her eyes go wide with shock. 'That's more than I expected.' She runs her fingers through her wild hair again. 'I cannet cope with this at the minute. You'll tell us if they do anything again?'

I nod. *Aye right*, I think.

'Don't you listen to all that rubbish about needing a dad. You're a good boy and you've had Granda. He's the best dad anyone could've asked for. You gan up and play your fiddle again if you want. I'll wash up. You want to sound good for that audition.'

I hadn't thought of it as an 'audition'. Granda will be dead disappointed if they tell me I'm rubbish.

I finish the last mouthful of me pasty. It's gone cold.

It's really hot and there's no air in me room, but I keep the window shut so nobody hears me. The sound of the fiddle echoes around the darkness but it doesn't make me feel happy like usual.

I hear Mam's phone ring so I stop and stand there, listening. I don't even know why cos I cannet really hear owt. She comes in, her face all twisted up.

'I've gotta go back up there,' she says. 'It's his breathing . . . he's really not doing too well.'

'I'll come.'

She shakes her head. 'No Archie. You look shattered. I'll tell him you're practising for tomorrow. Mebbe that'll settle him. The nurse said he's been having nightmares, like he's down in the pits again. And he's been callin' for your dad.' Her voice cracks. 'It'll be so sad if he never sees his son before . . .' she stops. 'Never mind, you get on. It's your chance and Granda wants so bad for you to take it.'

Before *what*? Before it's too late. That's what she's talking about, or *not* talking about. It's like a brick smashing on me head – Granda might not get better. That's why she wants me scumball dad to come back, to say goodbye and make it right between them. I sit on the edge of the bed, the fiddle hanging loose in me hands. I didn't think things could get worse. Pictures whirl in me head – the Robsons, Deela sobbing like her heart would break, Granda trying to breathe, Mr Akthar saying we're not to see Deela . . . But Granda not getting better? Granda dying? No way.

I slam me hand against the door jam and feel the sting on me fingers. Mustn't break them or tomorrow will be off. I know I have to do it – not for the money, but to make Granda happy. But I feel dead mixed up. I don't know if I can do this. I don't think I can do this at all.

I stand in the dark, touch the fiddle where it's lying on the bed. Slowly I pick it up. I don't switch the light on, just play in the darkness, feeling moisture on me face. It must be sweat. I blink hard and lick me chin. I taste the salt – definitely sweat.

14

It's pitch black when I wake. I wonder if there's a power cut cos normally there's a bit of orange off the streetlights. I can hear a voice, rough and teasing. It's one of them Robsons and he's in the room! I jolt upright, listening hard. His voice is further away now and I cannet catch his actual words, but there's this strong smell, like a farmyard, and a tremendous clattering of something heavy rolling past. I cover me ears and put me hand out, touch rough walls running with water. *What the hell?*

BANG! The dark shakes and I clutch the wall. There's a spray of water and dirt raining down on me.

'God almighty!' a man's voice yells. I feel summat whack me forehead and suddenly I can see again. The orange light filters through the curtains and me head is stinging where I've smacked it off the edge of the shelf above the bed.

'Archie? You alright, pet?' Mam's voice comes through the wall. 'It's four in the morning! What you doing in there?'

'Bad dream,' I mumble. 'I'm OK,' I call.

She goes quiet again. I slump back down under the covers, rubbing me head. It's bad enough being hunted by the Robsons in the daytime, but now they're taking over the nights as well? My body takes a while to settle. I keep hearing the explosion, keep feeling the rough wall under me fingers. The smell of ponies, slurry and Pets Corner in the park. Summat Granda told us once pops into me head, about how in the old days the ponies lived down in the pits for months at a time, never saw the light. I try and hear the sound of his voice, before it got so thin and breathless. I drift into sleep again feeling like he's close to me.

When me phone alarm wakes me up, the room is bright with sunlight. I put me hand up – I've got a lump like a hen's egg on me head. There's a message from Deela.

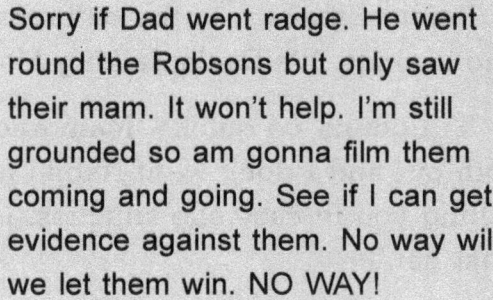

Sorry if Dad went radge. He went round the Robsons but only saw their mam. It won't help. I'm still grounded so am gonna film them coming and going. See if I can get evidence against them. No way will we let them win. NO WAY!

Deela

Great. Deela is now a one-woman vengeance team. It'll be a slow day for her – them Robsons probably won't even get out of bed till this afternoon. I'm pulling on me jeans when it comes to me – summat she can do that'll take a lot of time that I don't have. I message back.

Granda not so good. Asking for my dad. All I know is he went to London and disappeared off the face of the planet. Can you do your detective stuff and find him?

Archie

I don't expect she'll actually do it. I'm not even sure I want her to, but it'll keep Mam happy and give Deela something to think about that's not them Robsons.

Before I make it to the bathroom the phone rings. It's Deela, talking fast.

'I'm gonna be quick – Mam and Dad are both out and I don't want Nabila to know I'm calling you in case she snitches. I cannet trust her.'

'What are you ringing us for? You've never done that before.'

'I've never needed to. I'm just sooo bored already. Thought it would be cool to talk. What do you mean "find your dad"? Do you not know where he is?'

'I mean, if I did I wouldn't be asking you to look for him, would I? Mam's hassling me

134

to call him, but I just – I've got all this stuff on. I've got to get to this stupid audition right down in the Ouseburn this morning, and I want to see Granda in the afternoon.'

Deela's voice sounds so close, like she's leaning up against me, whispering in me ear. I picture her twiddling with the end of her plait, frowning as she thinks hard.

'Oh, Archie, I'm so sorry. Poor Granda. Last night I felt like I wanted to run away and never see my Dad again, but if I walked out, just left, I know he'd never give up on me. I definitely want to help. And so far, all I've got planned for today is to use Dad's CCTV to get evidence of the Robsons' gang coming and going. He has it pointed on our driveway for the car, but I've managed to reach out my bedroom window and sort of twist it so I can see if the Robsons come out their front gate. I can't do much if they go out the back way, though.'

'Deela, I'd hate to get on the wrong side of you.'

135

'Ha! Anyway, I can easy fit in looking for your dad. You need to tell us everything you know, though, like his full name, D-O-B, last address, number, workplace. Did he have a girlfriend? If yes, d'you know her address?'

'Er, he's Rob Bell and he's a builder . . . And it was London – I cannet remember where. It's not like I visited. Last number's not working and that's about it. I'll text the rest. He had a girlfriend, Janine. Don't suppose he's still with her, though. It's not his style. I cannet remember where she lived either. Brighton mebbe?'

'Janine from Brighton. It's not much to go on, is it? How can you know so little about your own dad?'

It's all right for Deela. Her family are close – so close it's suffocating but I don't say that. 'At least I know his name,' I say. 'Which is more than Kyle knows about his dad.'

There's a long silence and then a little whisper. 'Sorry. I will try, Archie. Send us anything you can find out. Gotta go now. Oh – good luck with this audition! You kept that

136

quiet. I really want to know . . . rats, Mam's back! Really gotta go.'

She hangs up. I toss the phone on to the bed and rummage round in the heap of clothes on my floor. I pull on jeans and a T-shirt. They're not *clean* clean, but I've worn worse. I head into the kitchen to grab something to eat and drink some juice straight out of the carton. Mam works in a bakery and we normally never run short of bread, but she's been so distracted we're down to the crust. I spoon some jam on to it and it's fine. Mam's already gone to work – early shift so she can see Granda in the afternoon. There's no sign of Kyle and I think I'm already a bit late. He never got back to me anyway, so I think I'm on me own.

I ease the tension on the bow. I get the fiddle out, and gently pluck out a little melody on the strings. I'm worried how hot the weather is. The wood of a fiddle is like a living thing – it shrinks and swells with heat and cold and dry and damp. I hope I can get it tuned OK when I get down to this studio – I'll look a right kid if I cannet. I put it back in

the case, which is old and battered but
Granda says the fiddle's older, handed down
in the family. It's in our blood. I touch the
wood gently then close the lid. I suck in a big
breath of air. *Right*, I think. *I don't care what
they think of me and the songs I play, this is
for you, Granda.* I head out to get it over with.

Tyler Richards is hanging round the corner,
leaning against the barrier that stops cars
going on to the Spinney wood. He looks at
me and smirks but I ignore him, walking fast
through the trees towards the Not-Library.
The city's boiling already, the gum on the
paths is sticky and I try not to tread on it.
Gadget Guy's climbing out of the white car.
Tash is in the driving seat, big sunglasses
pushed up high on her forehead. He waves
like he's calling me over. I'm gonna be late,
but I hesitate enough for him to think I'm
keen to talk to him.

'Off for a lesson?' He looks at me fiddle
case.

I cannet be bothered to explain so I sort of nod and say, 'I've got to get down the Ouseburn Valley.'

He smiles. 'Interesting place. I'm renting a flat down there. It's got so many layers of industrial archaeology. I could happily spend days mapping it.'

'Aye, right,' I say. Each to their own. 'I'd better get on,' I add. I know it's not his fault, but I don't think it's healthy to be seen with him. Particularly as Tyler Richards is floating around clocking everything we do. I glance back, catch a glimpse of him through the trees.

I start to jog down the main road, fiddle case bumping like crazy against me. I could take the bus but I cannet see anyone waiting, which means one's probably just gone and I don't want to hang around. If I really leg it I can make it nae bother – especially if I take the shortcut through all the parks and under the railway.

It's dead hot even though it's so early, and I feel sweaty already. I'm gonna stink when I get there but worrying about that makes me sweat more. The sky's a moody grey colour, no sun, just this weird heat. It feels like the whole city might explode. I stop once and look back and I cannet see anyone following me. *Howay, man – get on with it*, I say to myself. I'm just jumpy about everything.

I go down the path that'll take me under the railway lines to the Ouseburn Valley, me feet loud with a slight echo like double footsteps. I glance back again, but it's deserted. I wish I'd gone round and woken Kyle up and got him to come with me.

It's damp and green, trees closing in around me. I jog down a long run of concrete steps to the riverside, shaking me head to avoid the midgies and the flies. Gadget Guy's right though, the valley is interesting to look at – like a model that's had layers and layers of stuff added. It's this weird mix of country and city. There are streetlights stuck in among the trees and bushes, new blocks of flats and crumbling old buildings with the roofs of industrial units, and old pigeon lofts poking through the leaves – all squished together on a hillside so steep you could use it as a ski-run.

I checked where the studio was before I left, but I cannet remember now. I think of googling it but how hard can it be to find? I can see a skinny lad up ahead sitting on a fence, looking at some ponies in a small field. I guess I'll ask him if he knows where the studio is, but a soft clapping noise makes me turn and I see a flock of pigeons flapping and wheeling around the valley. When I look back, the boy's gone. Typical.

I go back down along a cobbled lane and over the Ouseburn River. The tide's out and the water is low. There are stones and mud, and a few small fishing boats, tipped on their sides, green weed hanging off their ropes, waiting for the water to come back in. There are no people around and the valley has a secret, closed feel, like everyone's hiding inside the old buildings, holding their breath and watching me wander round like a loser. Suddenly, I see a shabby old building with a big sign saying *Fogg on the Tyne's Sound Studio* over a scuffed blue door. I take a deep breath and rush myself straight in so that I don't change me mind.

I crash into a reception room and just stand there awkwardly. There's a girl with a nose ring and short red hair sitting at a desk. She looks at me and says, 'Archie Bell?' I nod, and she calls out, 'Jim, Archie's here. D'you want him straight through?'

A massive old guy comes out from another room. He's got all this white, curly tangled hair and he's wearing a scratty old T-shirt with a fat hairy belly hanging out. He's smiling.

'Nice to see a young lad interested in the old music,' he says. 'Not many younger folk players now. Been playing long?'

I nod.

'Wasn't it you I saw playing at Monument the other day?'

I nod again like a stupid nodding dog. Me hands are shaking, which isn't much good if you want to play well.

142

'Get your fiddle out, lad, and play whatever you want,' he says. I follow him out into a smaller room that's a proper studio with a sound deck and microphones. He chats on while I open the case, but I don't really hear a word of it. This is worse than busking. *If it wasn't for Granda . . .*

I picture Granda's strong hands moving over the strings, sure of every note. I put me bow to the fiddle and play the first tune that comes into me head. As I shut me eyes and let the notes come, it's like the old lads and lasses of the past are singing right in me head. At the end I can hear Granda's voice, young and powerful again, singing along with the fiddle. I don't care what this old gadgie with the hairy belly says, I don't care if he doesn't like it – I know Granda would be nodding his head and saying, 'Not bad, Archie lad, not bad!'

I open me eyes.

'Well done, Archie!' The old guy says, clapping his big furry hands. 'You're a natural, you're great. What else d'you kna?'

Me face feels hot. '"Byker Hill", "The Watter of Tyne", "Four Pence a Day" and other stuff.'

He asks me to play a few more so I do, his feet stamping every so often, driving the rhythm home. When I'm done, he beams, rubbing his hands together.

'Great! I'm sure your mam told you that I'm wanting to record some of these great old tunes and I'm lookin' for new young players to liven up the band a bit. A few old gadgies are droppin' out and I want to keep the music alive, pass it on, like.'

'That's what me Granda wants, n'all,' I say. 'He taught me.'

'You interested then? Let's see how we sound together.'

He gets his guitar and we play. He's really good, like the instrument's part of his body. He knows all the songs I know and loads more. After about an hour I just want to bring a duvet here, move in and never leave. The only thing that bothers me is how much

Granda would've loved to be in on this, to sit and play with this guy.

Fogg puts down his guitar. 'I've got a new young singer – a girl with a great voice – and some of us old timers as well. I reckon it's shaping up nicely.' He scratches his head through his bushy white hair. 'What do I need to tell you? If you're interested, first rehearsal's next week – usually Tuesday nights. We'll see how it goes, mebbe do some recording. We've got some gigs lined up and you'll get about thirty quid for each one. We cover costs then the rest is equal shares. Alright? You'll find me a man of me word.'

'Thirty quid?' I say. Just for playing a few songs?

'I know it's not much,' he says, like I'm complaining, 'but I have to pay for the van, petrol, and there'll be six in the band. You won't make your fortune playing folk music, but it's a great life.' He laughs a big laugh that makes his belly jiggle. 'So, who's your granda that taught you all the old songs?'

'You'll not have heard of him, he only played in the house,' I say. 'Bill Bell.'

'Get away! Well, I never. Old Bill Bell, eh? That's a blast from the past. I heard him play, oh, must've been back in the seventies and eighties. We all gigged the same pubs and social clubs. Mostly gone now – the people and the places.' He sighs. 'I heard his wife died and he never played again. Just hung up his fiddle and gave up. And he's your granda? He's done a good job with you, mind.'

A wave of sadness hits me.

'D'you want a tea? Coffee? Pop? You must be dry after that.'

I follow Fogg out to the reception where the girl with the nose ring is tapping away at a computer. I settle for a glass of water and a biscuit and we go back into the studio so he can show me the sound deck. It's awesome – like something you could fly a plane from. *This is it*, I think. *This is what I want to do when I leave school.*

'Jim?' The girl's head comes round the door. 'Next one's here.'

He sighs. 'Gotta get on, Archie,' he booms, then drops his voice to a shout. 'Got some wannabe singer come up to do a demo. They all want to sound like Beyoncé or Adele, or the next big thing – get on TV and all that rubbish.' He reaches out and grabs me hand and shakes it, which is kind of awkward. 'Great meeting you, Archie, been a pleasure. See you Tuesday, seven-ish, right here for first rehearsal. You can meet the others. Great.'

The girl ushers me out past a tall lad with a little goatee beard who is waiting, looking proper annoyed. I'm not convinced he'll want to sound like Beyoncé.

I'm grinning my head off as I step through the blue, scuffed door. I cannet wait to see Granda's face light up when I tell him everything.

15

Once I'm out the studio, I'm amazed how fast the morning has gone by. Outside, pigeons are going round and round in the sky, wheeling and dipping, invisible grey one minute and then – as they turn together all synchronised – silver-white against dark clouds. The sky is a strange, heavy grey-purple colour as if it's evening rather than only two o'clock – hot and airless. I've gotta get home. I'll tell Granda about the scooter plan, I think, and how with thirty quid each gig we'll make that scooter happen. It'll give him a boost.

I stand in the lane feeling like I'm buzzing and check me phone in case Mam's left a message. There are loads of long messages from Deela on the group chat and a few short ones from Kyle. I stand there a moment, the heat wrapping round me, like a weird, thick blanket.

The first one is from Deela, at about ten a.m.:

D Deela

> Hope audition goes good! Working hard on dad detection. Does he have a middle name? Sooo many Robert/Rob/Bob/Robbie/Bobby Bells in the world. Pity Granda wasn't more out there with naming him.

D Deela

> Just asked my cousin in London what she'd do to find someone. She said Asian local radio. But that'd probably only work if you were looking for someone who listens to Asian radio. Haha. Gonna try it!

D Deela

> I've put a shout out and sent it to loads of radio stations. London and national. Thinking of setting up a business: Adila A1 Detection Agency!

Deela

Do you know how many building companies there are in London? Your dad's definitely a builder, right? If he's like a car salesman I will screeeam. Let me know soooon before I email the next twenty companies

Deela

KYLE WHERE ARE YOU? You're not in an audition, so you should be helping me too. Just saying.

Deela

Just seen them Robsons are up and out. It's early for them. Kyle MESSAGE ME!

Kyle

Slept in. Mam's not home.

Deela

Get down the Ouseburn and find Archie! What will you do when you have a job and your mam's not there to wake you up?

Kyle

Wont be any jobs by then cos of AI. You comin 2?

Deela

Er . . . I'm grounded! Never mind Artificial Intelligence, you need to use some natural intelligence. Go meet Archie. The Robsons are out. EARLY. That is SUSPICIOUS. Only if you see them, don't let them see you. Have you got anything you could wear as a disguise?

There's a bit of a time gap and then another string of messages.

Kyle

Not seen them.

Deela

Dur! Go to the studio and meet Archie!

Kyle

Where is studio?

I laugh because even if he finds it, I won't be there. Poor Deela. She's obviously really suffering. I decide to call her and tell her the audition went good.

'Oh, Archie,' she says. 'Sorry, I saw the Robsons leave early and freaked thinking they might be after you. You OK?'

'Aye, I'm fine,' I say, suddenly a bit tongue-tied.

'That's a relief. I've sent Kyle to meet you but he's being useless today. Is your audition thing done? Did it go OK?'

I take a deep breath in, feeling like I might be breathing for both of us she's talking that fast.

'I'm just walking back. Yeah, it went . . .' I cannet find the words. 'Good,' I finally say. 'Really good. I forgot to be scared.'

'That's brilliant! What's it actually for?'

'To be in a band. I mean, it's not a cool band that people've heard of. They play folk music, like, the stuff I play. But Fogg – he runs the studio – he liked me playing. Says he'll pay us thirty quid for every gig.'

'Amazing! See, me and Kyle have always known you're good. Much better than some of them kids at school who show off at concerts. You really deserve this, Archie.'

I go through an alleyway away from the studio, phone jammed to me ear, me mind full of music and Deela's voice.

'Anyway,' she goes on, 'I think Dad's getting over being angry. First thing he said this morning was, "You do something for your family, Adila" and hands me a bottle of car cleaning stuff and a bucket of sponges to wash his car, like it's a punishment. I don't really mind doing it, though I've had to take a shower just to cool off.'

Deela's good at the full-on valet thing. When you run a taxi you can't have tissues and bits of crisps in the back seat like in normal people's cars. Customers want the cars to be as clean and shiny as a brand new one. Mostly Mr Akthar spends a lot of time doing that stuff but Deela helps sometimes.

'It was the perfect opportunity for some surveillance work. And now Dad's come back for lunch and he's given us fifteen quid for doing it.' She mimics Mr Akthar so well it's like he's on the phone. '"You go to the mall tomorrow with Nabila and buy a present for your mother. It's safer at the mall – cameras, security guards – no trouble".' She laughs. 'I'll save some for the scooter fund. And who knows, if I'm the perfect daughter for a few days mebbes he'll change his mind about me being grounded. That's the good thing about Dad – he's never radge for long. Plus, it's less than two weeks till we're back at school.'

'Cannet wait,' I say with added irony.

'Well at least it's something to do, and if I'm still grounded I'll get to see you all.'

I hear another voice – Nabila. 'Deela, have you seen outside? How dark it is? Weird! It's like it's night in the daytime.'

'Go away! I'm not talking to you. Can't you see I'm busy?' There's a pause where she obviously realises she shouldn't let Nabila know it's me she's talking to.

Nabila's voice comes loud and clear. 'Deela, even if you weren't hurt, no girl should put up with boys grabbing them. You can't keep it a secret just because you think it'll upset Mam and Dad. You'll thank me when you're properly grown up.'

I hear a door slam.

'Urgh!' Deela says. 'You're so lucky you don't have an annoying sister in your life.'

I change the subject to distract her.

'Any progress on the search for me dad? He was definitely a builder last time I heard. And a scumbag. Personally, I don't mind if we never find him.'

'Well, it's not about you, is it?' she says. 'Good job he is a builder cos I've messaged tons of London building companies and I'm only up to ones starting with G. You have no idea,' she says, 'NO IDEA how many there are. It'll probably take us a week to get to the end of them. If he works for one beginning with S I'll scream! Hey, get this though – you'll laugh. I got a reply – sooo exciting! Only it said, "Enter postcode for a quote for a house extension!"'

I'm hurrying along the empty street, listening to Deela's voice, not paying much attention to anything else, when I turn a corner and see a whole group of people all standing by the entrance to a great big iron gate. There's a woman with a clipboard talking, but everyone's peering up at the sky. It's worth watching, n'all. I've never seen it such a weird purple colour.

'I'm sooo hot,' Deela is saying. 'And Nabila's right – look how dark it's getting. I think it might chuck it down soon. You better get the bus quick if you don't want to get soaked.'

'Aye,' I say. 'I will.'

I need to cut the call and run, only there's this awkward pause.

'So, where are you now?' she says and I can tell she wants us to keep talking. I guess she's bored. I hoist the fiddle case higher and walk faster.

'Headin' towards the road,' I say. 'There's people, waiting . . . not sure what for.'

The woman with the clipboard has one of them high, clear voices like a teacher you just can't help hearing.

'Welcome to the Victoria Tunnel,' she says, 'where the coal from the pits was carried down to the Tyne.'

'I'm next to a tunnel,' I tell Deela. 'Wouldn't mind exploring that, but I bet you have to pay. It would be more fun to come on our own and play the fiddle to hear the echoes.'

'It would sound amazing in a tunnel,' Deela agrees. 'But that's probably not allowed.'

'Mmm. I don't suppose it's easy to get into, either.'

The tour party all go in and the woman turns to lock the gate. There's a shout and I stop and look back. It's just some old bald man, running. He's late for the party. He catches up and they all disappear into the darkness as the gate swings slightly. She's forgotten to lock it behind her. I hesitate – I *could* have a quick look? But Granda's waiting. I hitch up the fiddle case again. It's hot and slippery in me sweaty arms. The air's that close I feel like I'm suffocating and sweat drips down me back.

'Deela, I'll call you back later,' I say as I hear a yell.

'Howay, Archie, man!'

I turn and a skinny lad is racing down the hill. It's the strange boy from the park in his baggy long shorts and battered leather boots.

'Watch out!' he yells.

I jump out of me skin as someone drops down from a high wall right in front of me – tall, red-headed, grinning.

'No! The Robsons!' I blurt down the phone.

'What? Archie? What's that?' Deela says.

How did they know where I was? I bet it was Tyler Richards! He must've followed me and told them.

'They're here,' I say. Robson One laughs as I turn to run back to the studio but Robson Two is behind me, already blocking the way. The sky is suddenly even darker, like it's night. Me eyes shift, searching for a way out. I'm holding the phone tight in one hand, the fiddle case in the other. Deela's voice is a tiny squeak a long way off, but I have to concentrate on the twins.

I slip the phone into me pocket.

'You again,' Robson One says, smiling. 'Everywhere I gan there you are, fiddle boy. Gettin' in me face.'

Liar, I think but I don't say anything. The lad from the park skids down the cobbled lane and stops by the tunnel gate. The Robsons shoot a glance at him and Robson One laughs.

'I see you've traded in one pathetic little sidekick for another. What the hell's he wearin'?' He points at the lad's long baggy shorts, his bare legs sticking out of the old leather boots. 'Another weirdo like you!'

The lad doesn't react, just stands and watches from a few feet away. I glance at him and he grins, like it doesn't matter what anyone says about him. I feel bad for him. We're probably both gonna get thrashed.

Robson One takes a swig from a bottle of something he probably shouldn't be drinking. 'D'you wanna sell that thing?' he says, poking the fiddle case. 'I hear you can get a lot for a fiddle.' I stare at him, trying to work out what he's planning. The Robsons don't *buy* anything.

'It's old – not worth owt,' I say, which is true. I grip it tighter.

'It's worth more than money,' the lad from the park says.

'Ha!' Robson One says. 'Funny man. Nowt's worth more than money. You should sell it, buy yourself some protection. You and that lass.' The way he says the word lass makes it sound dirty.

Robson Two laughs and echoes him. 'Protection. Aye. She'll need it, won't she Bry? Her old man come round last night, givin' our mam grief—'

Robson One talks over him. 'Lucky for him we were out. Busy night, last night. People like him shouldn't even be in this country, you kna' that, don't you? They're illegals, takin' our jobs.'

Illegal – they'd know all about what that means. I don't say, 'What jobs? Working in the prison laundry?' though it flashes through me head. *Keep your mouth shut*, I think, *don't make it worse*. But I'm like a rat in a trap – no way out.

Robson One smiles. 'Not that he'll have a job when we finish with his car. We've got plans for that.'

Me mouth's dry and I don't think I can talk; like you can reason with them anyway. I try not to stare at them. I'm gripping the fiddle case so hard me knuckles shine white in the strange light. The park lad steps forward like he'll protect me, only he's that small and skinny I cannet see him being much use.

'Yous are just big bullies,' he says. Like that's gonna help.

'Leave it,' I say quietly. 'You don't know them!' I feel bad for him, getting involved in this. If only the tour group would come out the tunnel, but they don't. I try to walk away like this is normal, but I cannet. The twins block us in from either side.

Robson Two gives a giggle that makes the hairs on the back of me neck rise.

Robson One says, 'You gotta be careful round here. These roads,' he points at the cobbles in the lane, 'are proper rough. Someone like you could trip and mebbe,' he pauses, 'fall and,' he reaches towards the fiddle case, 'smash summat.'

I cling to the case but he snatches it as Robson Two grabs me arms.

'I'm warnin' ya!' the boy from the park shouts.

Robson One just laughs. He flicks open the case and pulls out the fiddle. 'Ya kna', we could look after it for you – oh no!' He fakes a drop, the fiddle sliding through his fingers before he catches it by the scroll.

'Good catch, Bry,' Robson Two says, pulling me arms tight behind me back.

That's when I lose it. Granda trusted me and I'd rather die than let them get it. I shove away from Robson Two but he's bigger, and he lifts me up so I'm dancing on me toes like a puppet on strings. I start to yell. Robson One dangles the fiddle in the air, swinging it, laughing. He's gonna smash it. I lash out with me feet and twist and kick out at Robson Two. Me foot connects with the place no lad ever wants someone's foot to connect with and he goes 'Ooof!' and lets me drop to the floor as he bends over, swearing.

The park lad pulls me up and I get me balance. I try to grab the fiddle off Robson One but he throws it up into the air. As both me and park lad jump for it, I sense danger behind us.

'NO, Bry! He's not worth it!' Robson Two shouts and almost at the same moment, something smashes on to me skull.

Sparks blaze as a dark wave of fierce black water throws me off me feet. There's a rush of heat, a shiver of cold. A white light flashes and the image of the twins prints on to me brain: one, grinning, a glint of sharp teeth and the other, his face crumpling, like a scared little bairn.

CRASH! The world splits with lightning. Rain drums fiercely on us as I slowly slide, down, down into pain and darkness. The fiddle . . . where is it? I hear Granda's breathing, that awful rasping.

'It's gone, Granda, it's gone!' I scream.

The breathing stops. There's only black silence.

16

The doorbell rings and Archie's mam steps into the Akthars' hallway.

'Shazia, I'm sorry to come round after what your husband said yesterday, but I'm worried sick. Granda's taken a turn for the worse. He's been begging for Archie but I cannet get through to him.'

'Come into the kitchen,' Mrs Akthar says. 'I'll put the kettle on.'

'Archie had an audition this morning. He's been out ages and he's not answerin' me calls. It's not like him to just disappear when it's visiting time at the hospital. I cannet get hold of Kyle, either. I never used to worry about them but since that trouble with them twins it's made me feel . . .' She gives a big

165

sob. 'I know I shouldn't've come, only I couldn't think who else to ask. Your Adila's been such a good friend to him. Would she know where he's gone?'

'It's OK,' Mrs Akthar says. 'Too much on your plate with Granda so ill. An audition? He's a clever boy with his music. I know he didn't mean harm with the busking.'

There's the sound of water filling the kettle and the two women are silent for a moment, feeling the heavy heat in the house.

'So hot today!' Mrs Akthar gets milk out of the fridge, finds mugs. 'Adila's grounded. She won't know, but I'll ask her. I'm sure he'll be home soon.' She pokes her head out of the kitchen door to call up the stairs. *'Nabila? Adila?* GIRLS! COME DOWNSTAIRS!' She stares wonderingly out of the kitchen window. 'It's so dark out there! What is happening?'

'Maybe an earthquake or the end of the world?' Nabila says, drifting into the room. 'I'm sooo hot. This isn't normal, right?'

There's a flash like a strobe light, bright white. The house shakes with a huge rumble of thunder and Nabila screams.

'Nabila – stop the drama and go get the washing in!' Mrs Akthar says as rain starts slamming down outside.

'Why me?' Nabila argues as Mrs Akthar thrusts a washing basket into her hands and pushes her out of the back door.

'Oh my word,' Archie's mam says, staring out of the back doorway and across the garden. 'Look at it! What if he's out in this? He'll be drenched! Wait! Is that him and Kyle?'

Mrs Akthar stares hard as well. Two figures are running across the Spinney, barely visible through the torrential rain.

'I think it's that Joshua, the archaeologist, and his tall girlfriend. I hope they find shelter. Have sugar in the tea,' Mrs Akthar says. 'Good for shock. Try not to worry.'

The door bangs and Mr Akthar comes in followed by Nabila laughing hysterically. She drops a plastic basket of clothes on the floor. Her father grabs a tea towel and rubs his wet hair.

'No, no, use a proper towel! Nabila – go get your father a proper towel. And call Adila down. Ugh! This washing is soaked through!'

Nabila stands, hands on hips. 'What about "thank you, Nabila"? It was like standing in a full-on shower out there – look at us, I'm dripping! Why didn't you ask Deela to get the washing in?'

The kitchen door flies open and Deela runs in and stops abruptly. 'Mrs Bell!' she says. 'I didn't know you were here.'

CRASH! Thunder rips through the air.

'So loud!' Deela says.

'At least you didn't get sent out to get soaked in it!' Nabila shakes her wet hair and combs through it with her fingers. 'Look at me!'

'Shut up Nabila – it's Archie!'

CRASH!

'Aaargh!' Nabila screams. 'Did you see that flash? Like an atomic bomb! And the rain, it sounds like bullets!'

Mrs Akthar points at Nabila. 'Not helpful! Now, no arguing, Nabila – go! Get a towel! Get two towels!'

'Like it matters when the world is ending!' But she runs out and up the stairs anyway.

Deela clasps her hands together. 'Listen! Please, don't be mad at me. It's Archie, Dad, I was just talking to him on the phone. *Please* don't be mad, it's important! I think he's hurt. We were talking, then he said the Robsons were there and it went all muffled, like a bum call, only there was shouting – and now his phone's just gone dead!'

'Oh my God,' Archie's mam whispers.

'I said to stay out of trouble!' Mr Akthar says.

'Baba,' Deela says, using the name she used for him when she was little. 'Baba, Archie's hurt!' Her voice is breaking.

CRASH!

169

'I'm ringing the police,' Archie's mam says, fumbling with her phone. 'Oh no, there's no signal!'

Mr Akthar looks at Deela and sighs. 'I could drive down, look for him.'

Another flash of lightning. Every little detail in the room stands out, vivid and clear – the kettle, the calendar on the wall, the jar of coffee on the work surface. Then it's dark again. The thunder rolls, and everyone stares out of the window over the back garden and towards the Spinney. The trees are bending in the wind, leaves swirling in the air. The ground is a lake of water.

'Towels!' Nabila says, coming back into the room and throwing a bright pink one at her father. 'Hey, sis, what's wrong? Don't cry.'

'Allah the merciful,' Mrs Akthar murmurs, grabbing Deela into a hug. She pulls free, but holds on to her mother's hand for a moment.

'I think we need all the prayers we can get right now,' Mrs Bell says as the lightning flashes.

There's a crack of thunder and it rolls on, a mighty voice. A huge, city-wide angry voice.

'Adila, do you know where Archie is?' her dad asks.

'He was down the Ouseburn, but I don't know exactly. Near a tunnel!'

Mr Akthar frowns. 'We will go. Wherever he is, it can't be a good place.'

I dunno where I am. Me cheek's throbbing and it scrapes painfully against the rough ground as I try to move. Everything's soaking wet, rain like sharp stones battering me. Someone's pulling me, urging me up.

'Howay, man, Archie! It's me, Billy. Get up! Hurry! The watter's comin'!'

Billy. The boy who saved Granda's life – that's his name. He was right once before and so I try to lift myself, but me head feels like a weight is tying it to the floor and me belly jumps into me mouth. I chuck up, but he ignores it.

'Howay,' he urges again, hauling me up. Me brain does a fierce roll in me head and bangs against me skull. Suddenly, I remember everything. I sink back to the ground.

'Me fiddle . . . them Robson lads.'

'Scared off! I divvent think you'll see them bad lads again,' Billy says. 'Took one look at me and legged it!' He laughs.

Rain slides down me face and drips off the ends of me hair. I give a howl of rage and misery.

Billy lifts me to me feet, his skinny body amazingly strong, and half-carries me to the entrance of the tunnel. There's a flash of light that blinds me and the pain in me head is fierce.

He props me up by the iron gate and steps into the tunnel's entrance.

'Comin'?' he says.

'But they took it, they're gonna smash it.' I'm crying. Spew and snot drip off me face, and I collapse down on me knees into the wet and slide down into the water, pooling on the concrete.

Kyle is suddenly skidding down the hillside towards us, like he's surfing the concrete. 'Archie, man! What the hell did they do to you?' His head is as wet as a seal's and he can barely see out of his glasses cos of the rain.

'They took Granda's fiddle!' I shout, bawling me eyes out like a little bairn.

But Billy, standing in the dark of the tunnel, lifts his arm and I see the fiddle hanging from his hand.

'Billy!' I shout.

Kyle stops dead like he's been hit. He's got this hard frown on his face as he stands in the pouring rain. 'It's me, Archie,' he says. 'Me, Kyle!' But it's like I'm seeing him through a dirty screen. His voice comes to me, far off, like he's in a dream – not real at all. I feel me body crumple down, down, down and me head smacks into the water.

'Would I let that happen? See! Safe and sound!' Billy's voice comes through a fog of noise – the crash of thunder, the sound of the rain drumming on the ground. I stagger back to me feet.

'Howay, man, come on! The others are waiting.' He puts his arm around me again and half carries me into the tunnel. I focus me eyes. The fiddle is hanging from his hand and it's whole and looking like he's given it a polish, though I dunno how he could have. The rain slams against the entrance and pours over the tunnel floor. I can taste sick in me mouth and when I touch me head it's wet and sticky. I look at me hand – blood.

Kyle's jumbled voice shouting about ambulances fades away and drifts off into nothing. Billy keeps pulling me, into the tunnel entrance.

'Kyle?' I whisper, but he's not following. I don't want to leave him behind, but Billy urges me on. I hear the metal gate slam behind us. I stagger along beside Billy as we head up the tunnel, away from the sound of the storm, deeper and deeper into the darkness.

*

175

We walk on and on with his tough, thin arm grabbing me and helping me over rough patches. I feel sick with tiredness and me head has hammers going at it inside. He stops and messes on for ages, making a scraping noise. I slump down on to the floor and close me eyes.

'I just wanna sleep,' I say.

'No, we need to keep gannin. The others are waitin' on us . . . see, the flint'll strike – there now!' There's a small flash and a flicker of light. He's got a candle but it doesn't help much.

'Use your phone, man,' I say, struggling to find mine in me pocket, but me clothes are so wet everything's stuck together. Mebbes I dropped it? How will I tell Mam I've lost me phone? 'At least we've got the fiddle,' I say under me breath.

The tunnel is made of small red bricks and is curved but high enough to walk upright. Staring down, the pattern of the bricks makes me eyes dizzy. I wonder where the tour group people are. The floor gets rougher and harder to walk on and when I put me hand out to save myself from falling, the walls are just rock – bumpy and sharp on me fingers. We come to a crossroads and the tunnel narrows and grows lower and lower till I cannet walk upright and I bang me head against the wooden logs that hold up the roof.

'What about health and safety?' I mutter, stumbling after him. 'The roof's too low . . .' I think about the tour group again. Have we passed another exit? I feel like I've walked miles, right across the city.

'Where does this tunnel end?' I say. 'Can I get a bus back from the other end? I don't want me fiddle to get wet now the case is gone. I bet they just chucked it away.' I'd be angry, only I'm too exhausted.

Billy doesn't say much, just keeps moving a bit too fast until suddenly he stops and I bump into him.

'I need to get out. This is making me feel . . .' I stop talking and throw up again. Sick and dizzy. It's like the roof's falling in on me. I feel like I'll never see daylight again, like there's no air. A wave of panic rises up. 'Get me out!' I shout. 'I've got to get out!'

Billy crouches in the dark. I can just see the bottom of his chin and the strange shadows of his face in the light of the tiny candle he has lit.

'Archie, shhh. Take deep breaths, man. In two, three, four, hold it . . . out two, three, four . . .'

I try to gulp the air, sweat pouring down my back.

'No . . . air,' I say, but he keeps up with the counting, breathing with me. In, out, in, out. How come you never think about breathing till you cannet?

'Slower,' he says. 'Slow it down – it'll pass. It's natural to feel the world's on top of you down here. It is. But you'll get used to the feelin' of the weight above. There now – better? Hold this – it'll help.' He hands me the fiddle and just the feel of the wood in me hands calms me. He's saved it. I cannet believe he's saved it.

'How did you . . . ?' I start to ask, but then
the words are lost again and I just sit
stroking the fiddle. 'I've gotta get out of
here,' I try to explain. 'I need to take the
fiddle to Granda and tell him about the band
and everything.'

Billy puts his thin, strong hand on me
shoulder and grips me hard.

'The fiddle's where it needs be, Archie.'
He's so close I can see the shine of his eyes
reflecting the tiny light of the candle. 'It'll be
a shock for you, man, but there's no way out.
When we were diggin' at the coal face it
started to bulge. We knew we were close to
the abandoned workin's – Heaton Banks – at
the bottom of the valley. They closed that
seam of coal down years back when it
flooded bad. But we thought it was safe
enough working where we were.' He rubs his
face with his grimy hand and I see his
knuckles are scraped and bleeding.

'You what?' I whisper. 'What d'you mean,
there's no way out? We came in, so we can
get out, right? And how can you be working
in the mine? There's no pits round here now

– Granda says they've all gone.' Just saying his name brings a wave of panic over me. 'Stop messin' about!' I shout. 'I've gotta get back!'

'Archie, I swear to you,' Billy says. 'The Heaton Main seam gave way three days ago now and the watter's come rushing through. I divvent kna who got out alive but me and me da and some of the men, we've found a safe place and we're waiting to hear them picks digging for us, to get us out. But the lads get really down. Divvent look at us like that, Archie, man! When I saw the fiddle I knew you needed help, and we needed help, too. Music in the dark. That's what we need to keep our spirits up till they rescue us. I knew you'd be the man to help us – one good turn, eh?'

'What?' I say. 'Why me? How?' But he doesn't answer. The flicker of candlelight makes the dark around us blacker. I pull myself up, feeling like I'm frozen in time. Or flying through time – I cannet tell the difference.

'Hey,' he says as I lose me balance and crash down into loose dirt and stones. 'You need to eat. We've got food – we cannet feed the horses so old man Johnson's killed one and we've got horse steaks all round. We'll not starve. Just a little bit further then we can rest and eat with the others.'

'No,' I say. 'Please, I've got to get back . . . Mam and Granda, they'll be waitin'.'

Voices are calling and there's a low glow of light. I stumble towards it, like it's pulling me out of the blackness. I think mebbe it's the tour group, but in my heart I know it's not. This isn't the brick-built tunnel it should be. This isn't anywhere a bunch of tourists would walk. I'm bent double trying not to brain myself on the low ceiling.

Slowly Billy helps me along and we finally come out into a cavern that's wider and higher, with pinpoints of wavering candlelight. A crowd of faces peer at me out of the shadows. It's hard to tell how old they are as their faces are blackened with dirt but as they speak, I realise some are just young lads.

181

One of the older men steps forward.

'Da,' Billy says. 'This is Archie. He's brought us the fiddle.'

'I'm Joe,' Billy's dad says, touching me shoulder. He has a deep, slow voice. 'Are ye hurt, lad?'

I feel sick and shivery, but I shake me head.

Joe turns to the group. 'Look what Billy and the lad, Archie, have brought us – a tune to go with our dinner. What more could a man want?'

'To see the good sun and the light again,' a rough voice comes out of the darkness. 'And not to have to listen to you praising God in this cesspit.'

'Shut yer mouth, Rab Robson,' says another voice.

No! Not another Robson to deal with! I take a gulp of air, remembering that they hit me on the head. Mebbe I'm in some kind of coma. Or worse – mebbe I'm dead.

'Billy?' I say. 'Am I dead?'

'We're all dead men here,' says Rab Robson. 'No hope for us miners when a pit floods. D'yous really think the owners'll rescue us? Yer fools to hope!'

'Shut it, Rab,' another shouts. 'Look at the lad, he divvent kna if he's comin' or goin'.'

I sink to the ground, feeling the wet stone floor, rough under me hands. There's this thudding beat in me head. This has to be a dream, right? Just another nightmare. I try to jolt me body to wake myself up, but nothing happens. When I open me eyes I'm still here.

The place smells like farmyards, animals just like in the dream. Horses. I can hear them stamping nearby. Me stomach rolls as I finally catch up with what Billy said – they've started to eat the horses. I remember Deela saying how disgusting it would be to eat horse meat. This cannet be real. This *isn't* real, is it?

'Deela,' I say. I cannet bear that I'll never see her again. I will myself to wake up from this.

I put me hand in me pocket, pull out me phone. I can ring for help! It'll be OK. This isn't the past, this is now! I'm so relieved it still works.

The green glow of the screen lights up the tunnel. The men gasp and murmur, confused. One is saying it's 'an unholy light,' whatever that means.

Some of the men start to sing – sad, religious songs calling on God to save them from their troubles. It's too real to be a dream, but I cannet think about that. I focus on making a call . . .

Nowt.

I try to send a message but there's no signal. I feel myself choking up. I should've known there'd be no signal in a tunnel. And no signal in the past when there were no phones and no satellites whirling through space to help us.

Space.

I feel the weight of the ground above me, pressing down.

I sit holding the phone, staring at the
green light, the beautiful light. I look at the
messages from the real world. The last one
that had come was from Deela.

Deela

> Call us. Are you OK? We're looking
> for you.

I think of them all and feel this wave of
relief – they're looking for me! But the
mournful singing gets louder, full of sadness.
I touch the rocky wall. It's solid under me
hands. If this is real, if somehow, I'm down
in the mine, two hundred years back in time,
how will Deela and Kyle ever find me?

I take shallow breaths of the warm stench of
the mine. When Billy grabs me hand, his is
real; warm and alive. He puts the fiddle,
Granda's fiddle, to his chin and starts to
play. He doesn't stumble or falter and it's like
the instrument's his own. I know the first
tune and the second. Everyone gradually

joins in and some of the younger lads are banging a hammer on to a bit of wood, keeping time. Some start to stamp and there is a rattle of stones falling and dirt drifts off the ceiling on to our faces. I watch Billy's hands, moving over the strings. I'm so close I can see the strange marks on his fingers, like grey messages written in old pen or faded tattoos.

He hands the fiddle to me. 'Them marks,' I say. 'Granda has them on his hands n'all.'

Billy says, 'It's where the dirt and the coal dust gets into the cuts. You cannet get rid of it. The pit signs a man with its mark and you cannet wash them off, no matter how hard you try. It's, like, written into your skin.' He gives me the bow. 'There you are, settle yourself. Give us a tune.'

Just the feel of the fiddle calms me down. I pluck a string and the sound echoes round the rough cave. I think of Deela and Kyle and Granda and Mam. There's a pain in me chest, a feeling like I cannet breathe free, but I pull the bow across the strings and play. The voices rise and fall, the voices of all the

lads who know they're gonna die, singing in
the blackness as the dark watters rush
through the mine.

I know this isn't a dream. I know who
they are and I know there'll be no happy
ending. I've done the school projects.
Seventy-five men and boys, suffocated and
drowned in the Heaton Main Pit when it
flooded. How can I tell these eager faces that
they'll never see the Dene and the moor and
the sun and the sky ever again? They're
trapped and so am I. How can I bear to never
see family and friends again? Or walk the
parks and see the green of the trees? I
cannet look at the men's faces, so I close me
eyes and play on. When I stop the lads all
clap and cheer and a bottle is passed round
with some water that tastes as bad as it
smells. I take a sip as me lips are burning
with dryness, but it makes me stomach
heave again.

'The fiddle helps,' Billy whispers to me.
'Music makes things bearable. God knas I
needed you, as you and yer Granda needed
me.' He points to some sacks against the

wall. 'Here, wrap yourself in them and the ground'll not feel so hard. You rest,' he says. 'I'll take care of the fiddle. I'll never let it out me sight again – not till God closes me eyes on the dark for good.'

18

Mrs Akthar puts her arm round Archie's
mam, who collapses down and leans against
her. There's another flash of startling bright
light and the thunder rolls again. Everyone
stares at Mr Akthar, draped in shocking pink
towelling.

'Please, Baba,' Deela says. 'Something
bad's happened to Archie down there,
mebbe Kyle as well. I want to come with
you.'

He mutters something in Urdu under his
breath that only Archie's mam and Deela
hear, but only Deela understands. It is
'loyalty'.

'We go look for the boys.' He grabs his tea
and swills it down in one gulp. 'I will bring

Archie to the hospital,' he announces, 'to his grandfather. Mrs Bell, you go to the hospital – you need to be there. We won't let you down. Adila, get your raincoat.'

'Please ring us as soon as you find him,' Archie's mam says. 'I'll tell Granda he's comin'.'

Mr Akthar drops the pink towel on the kitchen chair and he and Deela leave before anyone can open their mouths to say anything else.

The rain is coming down like the chute of a water flume, the wind slamming the lids of the wheelie bins and bending the bushes flat to the ground. Deela and her dad jump into the car, already soaked to the skin. The thunder and lightning are constant and the windscreen wipers can't keep up with the rain.

'It's like monsoon rains in a movie where they have a machine that just pours water on to the set,' Deela says, leaning forward and peering through the windscreen.

Her dad is shaking his head with amazement. 'I've never seen anything like it in this country.'

The car slides a bit in the water, but Mr Akthar drives well. He cuts across the Coast Road, edges his way through the traffic slowed to a jam, turns down back alleys and through the terraces – knowing which ones are permanently closed and which ones can be a way through. All the streets of the city are in his head.

'Worse than I thought, the underpasses will flood,' Mr Akthar mutters. 'They're so low lying there is nowhere for heavy rain to go, you see. Bad planning in the 1960s. Those roads are death traps!'

'Dad, look out! See them cars – they're coming at us on our side of the road!'

Sirens blare as the city grinds to a halt, water flowing off the pavements and along the roads. It swirls at the drains but doesn't go anywhere.

'Soon this will be too deep for a normal car to drive through.' He gets round a small car already stranded in the water, but he's shaking his head again. 'I'm afraid my car will drown and if the electrics get wet we'll lose it. You need big four-wheel drives, higher off the road for this.' He pulls halfway on to the pavement and drives as far as he can, looking at the water gushing towards them. 'It's like a river,' he says quietly, 'flowing down to the valley. It seems to be draining down that way. I think we will leave the car here as this is the highest point of the road before it drops again. We'll walk from here. I shouldn't have brought you. Maybe I could leave you at your uncle's restaurant, we're close by—'

'There's no time for that,' Deela says. 'I'm trying Archie and Kyle again . . . Argh, still no signal! Can a storm knock out all the phone masts? It feels like the end of the world.'

'We leave the car here and hope for the best,' Mr Akthar says, pulling the handbrake up hard. 'Be careful getting out, Adila.'

They climb out into what looks like a stream churning its way down the road.

'So weird,' Deela says. 'Urgh, the water's freezing! Why's it so cold when it's summer? And there's so much rubbish!'

A small boy of about seven is screaming and sobbing as he wades through the water, following his mum who has a toddler on one hip and a bag of shopping hanging off her arm. The lightning flashes again and the boy stumbles and falls. Mr Akthar splashes through the rising water and hoists him up. Deela takes the shopping bag and they all push their way up the street that's now fast as a river and up round their legs. The woman points to a house.

'I should've stayed in the shop when the rain came, but we live so close . . .'

Dirty water surges through their tiny front garden, plant pots banging up against the brick wall and a child's plastic slide tipped on its side, bumping at the gate like it wants to get out. There's a step up to the house, which is just as well or the water would be swirling in their sitting room. The woman struggles to open the door while Deela holds the toddler, who clings to her for a moment with small, wet hands.

'Put blankets across the doorway,' Mr Akthar says. 'Rolled up, keep the water out. You will be OK?'

The woman gives them a quick smile – half relieved, half anxious – and pulls the door shut.

They wade on through water scummed with leaves and rubbish towards the edge of the hill. They dodge wheelie bins that float towards them. People are everywhere, like ants trying to salvage things, trying to get from one place to another. Cars float in the river roads.

'It's like an advert for disasters on the other side of the world,' Deela gasps. 'We've gotta find him.' She puts her lips together tightly, thinking, *don't cry, don't complain*.

They cross the next main road and head down the steep hillside, which has turned into a waterfall. There are fewer people down here, though faces peer out from studios and offices as Deela and her dad inch their way down the steep sides of the valley.

'We will not give up,' Mr Akthar says, glancing down before rubbing the rain from his eyes.

Police sirens scream in the distance and thunder shouts back.

19

I drift in and out of sleep with strange and heavy dreams. Deela comes to me in the darkness and I can feel her hand warm on me shoulder as she shakes me awake.

'You've gotta come back, Arch,' she says. 'Granda needs you.'

I try to hold on to her fingers but they slip away from me, turning to water in me hands. And then I really wake up and hear men calling out and grunting.

I'm in darkness, trapped in a mine. I bite me finger, really chomping down. It hurts. So mebbe this is real? Or just another layer of dreaming? Me head hurts n'all, and there's dried blood in me hair that itches and pulls. I hear a man screaming and swearing, yelling into the dark. One is praying out loud, terrible endless begging for the light, until someone bangs a hammer against the roof and shouts out.

It's Rab Robson. 'I swear on me mam's grave, I'll bring this bleedin' roof in if you divvent shut yer mouth.'

'Let the lad alone, Robson,' Joe says in his deep, calm voice.

There's moving of bodies and many people calling out. Me tongue feels furry, stuck to the roof of me mouth. I imagine a glass of iced, clean water out of a tap. Modern water that tastes of good fresh nothing. I can hear a horse desperately stamping and whinnying and me eyes well up. Why is it I can cry for a horse I cannet even see, but not for Billy or all them bodies breathing, sweating, praying?

I touch the fiddle by me side. Granda. He'll think I've decided not to come and see him. He'll think I've abandoned him. I turn away from the men and hold me breath. I want to sleep again, and wake up and be back in me room – everything normal.

But sleep won't come. The men have calmed down. I can hear them talking about being rescued.

'I've always said,' a voice says, 'there should be more than one shaft. If they'd sunk another shaft, we'd not be trapped like rats in a pipe.'

'They'll dig in from the old workin's, you'll see.'

'Haddaway, man. Will they heck. It's the old workin's done the damage. That watter's been building up there ever since that pit was lost – didn't have pumps fifty years back. Them new steam pumps are grand for keepin' the watter down. Aye, I tell yous this pit's one of the best, lads. There's summat to be proud of. No way will they let it go. They'll find a way to pump it clear, you'll see.'

Rab Robson shouts out in his rough voice. 'You can die in the best pit as easy as the worst. Trusting the viewer and the overman, trusting the coal barons to do right by us men – we're fools, we are. Livin' fools and dead fools.'

I try to remember all the things Granda told me and Kyle about the old days. The viewer who made sure fresh air came through the mine, the overman who checked if the pit was safe. And the coal barons who owned everything – the mine and the coal and the houses everyone lived in.

There's a silence broken by sighs and the sound of men shifting themselves and the scrape of metal on metal. I can hear the creaking of the wooden pit props holding up the roof. I try not to let the panic of knowing how much weight is above us take over.

'They could come at us from the other side,' a voice says, sounding like he knows they won't. 'If we could hear the picks we could start to work towards them.'

I sit up, me back against the wall. Billy is suddenly beside me.

'In the park, when you said to us to gan home, I thought it was luck,' I say. 'And when you saved the fiddle I thought it was more than luck, like a miracle.'

Billy settles himself down and I feel the wood of the fiddle against me bare arm.

I try to put me jumbled thoughts into words. 'I dunno how you can be out there in my time and trapped down here in this time? Or how you got me down here. But you saved Granda's life. Are you wantin' my life in return, is that it? Or am I meant to, like, save yous all?' I pause. 'Cos I dunno how.'

'Nah, Archie, man, it's not like that! Are you hungry?'

Me belly growls.

'Well, lucky I've got a bit of horse steak for you.'

I can hear the men chewing. The smell of the raw flesh makes me heave all over again and I shake me head.

'I still feel sick,' I say.

'You'll get over it. When your belly's sticking to your ribs and you're clammin' with hunger.'

Time seems strange – both slow and fast. There's nothing to do, but at the same time a whole life to live.

'I'm only just fourteen,' I say. 'It isn't fair if I die now.'

Billy nods. 'Aye, some are younger . . . it's harsh. But it's worse for the families when it's the older men. Lose me and Mam'll grieve, lose Da and she'll lose her house, her coal allowance and his wage.' Billy sighs. 'I'll find you some more watter to drink.'

I watch him move away into the shifting shadows. I've never thought of what it must have been like to know you'll never get out. I've never thought about how slow the time goes when you're waiting and hoping. I watch a lad about my age using a nail to scratch the top of a tin box.

'What you doin'?' I ask him.

'It's a message for Mam,' he says, 'I divvent want her to think I've never thought on her. I divvent kna what she'll do with me and Da and our George gone.' He carries on scraping away with the nail, though the candlelight is so pathetic he can barely see what he's doing. 'But she'll . . . know . . . I loved her.' He starts sobbing soundlessly, just his chest heaving up and down. The other men look away. I picture Mam standing in the kitchen, waiting for me. Only the door never opens and she never gets to see me again. There's a lump in me throat that makes it hard to speak, but I force myself.

'She'll know,' I say. 'Mams always know you love them, even if you never say it. They just know.'

We're silent for a while as he keeps working on the tin – scrape, scrape, scrape.

'I wish I'd been nicer to me mam,' I tell him. Out of the dark I feel his thin, dirty hand grab mine for just a moment. Neither of us says another word. He rubs his eyes then picks up the nail again and carries on scratching away.

'I love you' isn't very long – I wonder what else he's writing. I lightly pluck the strings of the fiddle, hear it talking to me gently. I'm glad when I hear Billy coming back with water. I'm so thirsty I actually take some, rubbing a bit on me lips then gulping a bit down, trying not to smell the taste of it. I see his eyes shine in the wavering light. He's grinning.

'I got it where it's fresh, drippin' through and runnin' off the wall – better than dippin' it out of the puddles on the floor.' He glances at me. 'I tell you what,' he says, crouching down, 'best way to get through this, is to put yourself somewhere else, out in the sunshine. I try to go walking in me mind, down the Dene and over the fields up at Freeman's Farm. I picture every step of the way, feel like I'm there with the trees and birds and flowers, feel the sun on me back. That's when I saw you and your little marra with the shaven head and the bonny dark girl. Is she your lass?'

'Nah, just a friend,' I say, digging me nails into me palms. What is 'just' a friend? She'll

203

probably fall for someone like Gadget Guy who's clever and going off to uni and that. To never see Deela again . . . I cannet talk about her without the big lump sticking in me throat so I change the subject. 'I still don't understand how you could be here trapped and yet there, in the park? And about Granda, being took bad. How'd you know?'

Billy shrugs and his shadow, cast on the wall, ripples across the rock. He picks up the fiddle, lovingly stroking the neck and picks out a little tune.

'Blood and watter,' he says. 'Blood and watter.'

20

'D'you kna this one?' Billy says, stroking the bow over the strings.

I don't. He plays it through twice and then hands me the fiddle. I copy him, making a few mistakes, correcting and playing a tricky run a couple of times. He starts to sing as I play to keep me right. This song is sadder than the others and it sounds older, I think. We take turns to play and sing it through three or four times until I know it.

'That's the song the mams sing when they lose their bairns,' he says when we finish – the last note just a vibration in the heavy air.

'Why did you even come and work in the pit?' I say. 'Couldn't you have done something – anything – else?'

'People like us – we've no choice.' He pauses. 'This pays our wage, puts food in our bellies. It's not such a bad life when you're strong and you work a good seam with a good viewer.'

'So what went wrong here?' I say, suddenly angry. This disaster wasn't natural, it was someone's fault.

'I divvent kna,' he says. 'The viewer tested whether the coal wall was safe, but the drift must've been thinner than he thought. When we cut in, the waste burst through from the old Heaton Banks pit and the watter flooded in and filled the tunnel. That was two days back. Some lads no doubt drowned where they stood. I'm hoping some got out. We were in a higher part and the watter's not reached here yet. . . but the tunnel's blocked and we cannet get out.'

'Can you not swim through the water? Get back to the exit shaft?'

Billy slaps his legs and laughs his head off. Some of the other men join in and I feel like an idiot.

'Nobody,' Billy gasps, 'nobody could hold their breath that long! The tunnel dips down and stretches a mile back to the pithead – it'll be full of waste and rock now.'

'An' who can swim?!' an older man says. 'Watter weakens your back till it's soft as a lily stalk. I've not been in watter since I was a tiny bairn in skirts an' I'm not about to start now.'

Skirts?! Did boys wear skirts two hundred years back?

'Give us another song, Billy,' a different voice shouts.

I give him the fiddle and he plays a tune that jigs and dances along. The next one I recognise. It's an old hymn Granda sometimes used to play. He'd sing some of the words, then sigh and put the fiddle away and take us out on a long walk down the parks to where the Ouseburn meets the River Tyne. By the time we got there he'd be back to his normal self.

A strong voice, Joe's voice, comes out of the blackness singing along.

I once was lost, but now am found

Was blind, but now I see . . .

I rub my eyes in the endless darkness.
We're all blind down here. The few candles
give weak pinpoints of light that just make
the dark around them thicker.

More voices join and the sound swells.

Through many dangers, toils and snares

I have already come

T'was grace that brought us safe thus far

And grace will lead us home

All but a few of the men join in. The lad
with the tin is weeping out loud now but
nobody says anything, they just let him. They
sing mournful words to God and I wonder if
God really exists. They don't seem to doubt
he does, even though no help has come – or
ever will.

'You divvent have to tell us,' Billy whispers in my ear when the last note fades away into silence and the men sit hunched with their thoughts. 'We kna hope is failing, that the watter's rising. We cannet hear the picks and shovels.'

'There's no happy ending,' I say, shivering.

'Never say that,' he says. 'There's never an ending, happy or not. It all just keeps on going, like a chain gannin round and round in a wheelhouse or a mule on a gin gan, or the river flowin' on and on.'

Rab Robson's rough voice cuts through. 'I'd like a bit of that Grace – she could lead me home alright!'

'Shut your big ugly mouth, Robson, or you'll gan to hell,' someone says.

'And I thought we was already there!' Robson rasps back. 'Mebbe if you give us summat a bit more ruddy cheerful to listen to?'

Billy shrugs and strikes up 'Byker Hill'. I know it well – it's one of Granda's favourites about the miner lads.

The men roar out the chorus, like they're drunk.

Byker Hill and Walker Shore

Collier lads for ever more . . .

Drunk on bad water and hope.

21

Although the rain is still heavy, the thunder and lightning are further away with longer gaps between them.

'It's easing off, I think,' Mr Akthar says.

'I see someone!' Deela shouts. A boy is running up the hillside, shouting for help, clutching something awkwardly in his arms – a box, no – a case. Fiddle shaped!

'Archie!' she shouts.

But it's Kyle, soaked to the bone, his head wet as a seal.

'They've killed him!' he cries out, holding up the case. 'They took his fiddle and then they killed him. I saw them running past me – they dumped it and I thought mebbe the fiddle would be in it, that I could save it, but it's empty!' He points away down the hillside. He suddenly sobs hard, 'Deela, I think Archie's dead! I pulled him out the water but he's slippin' away.'

Mr Akthar splashes on down the lane, Kyle right behind him. Deela is stone, not able to move. Archie dead? How is that even possible?

'No, it's not true!' she yells suddenly, coming back to life. She races down the hill, skidding and sliding, and catches them up at the metal gate to the old wagon way tunnel. It's open and just inside is a horrible humped up pile of clothes with a lolling pale face – Archie.

Mr Akthar crouches down, the dirty water slopping over them. Kyle gasps, 'Last thing Archie said, he called us Billy. He didn't even recognise us, then he just kind of collapsed. His head was in the water and there was blood everywhere.'

Deela pulls out her phone to ring for an ambulance but there's still no signal.

Kyle slumps to the ground, sobbing. 'I tried that, but nowt's working. I pulled him up so his head was out the water and I stayed with him hoping he'd come round. But he got colder and colder. In the end I *had* to leave him to get help. I didn't know what to do!'

'Is he breathing?' Deela says. 'Dad? He *must* be breathing.'

Mr Akthar puts his head close and lifts Archie, dripping water and streaked with dirt and blood. He tries to feel for a pulse in Archie's neck.

'Oh my God,' Deela whispers. 'Oh my God.' Her mind skips through every disaster movie she's ever seen, where you guess which character will die first and almost everyone is dead by the end. She pictures the band of heroes, the ones who make it through the horror and go to stand by the graveside where 'ARCHIE' is carved in big bold letters, just before the credits roll. But it's all wrong. It shouldn't be Archie's grave – he can't die. She won't let him die.

'*No*,' she says again.

'Archie, man!' Kyle's begging. 'Divvent be dead, man!'

Deela touches Archie's cold wet fingers that make that old fiddle of his sing. How can those stupid twins have done this to him? How can they just destroy all the good? How can the good *lose*?

'This isn't how the story's meant to end,' she whispers.

'Mind! Don't stand on the boy!' Mr Akthar says. There's a horrible long pause, then, 'OK, OK, he's breathing. We must get him under cover, get him warm.' He scoops Archie up, who slumps, limp in his arms, his hand hanging down and dripping water.

'What's that noise?' Kyle says as Mr Akthar hoists Archie on to his shoulder.

They listen hard; a distant siren, someone shouting from some warehouses, the sound of the rain hitting a metal roof, and then – low but clear – singing.

'It must be a radio,' Mr Akthar says as he starts to wade through the water. 'Maybe in a car that's been left when the flood came. It will drain the battery.'

Kyle tips his head. 'Weird kind of radio.' He hurries after them. 'It's creepin' me out. Sounds like what you hear on films when there's a funeral.'

'Quick,' says Mr Akthar. 'We don't want no funerals here!' He speeds up, Archie balanced on his shoulders, Deela trying hard to support his head.

'No way,' she says. 'Not on our watch.'

As they wade through the water, the low, mournful sound of the singing rises and falls.

I once was lost, but now am found . . . coming from who knows where.

22

I'm losing all sense of time. I sleep and dream I'm under the rustling green trees in the park with Deela and Kyle. I wake with wet cheeks that I scrub at awkwardly, then realise it's so dark and dirty no one can see if you've been crying.

Billy stirs in his sleep next to me. I wonder if he's dreaming of the exact same places as I am, with the same longing to be there in the light. I've no idea how long we've been here and when I tap me phone to see the comforting green light, the battery has gone flat. I scratch at me face and long to be standing in a hot shower, the dirt just washing away. I try to remember the smell of shower gel and shampoo. I'll never whinge on to Mam when she nags me to take a shower. That's if I ever see Mam again. I cannet even think about Granda.

There's the sound of sobbing and I peer through the gloom. There's a little kid, about seven years old, sitting against one of the wooden props that hold up the roof. His eyes look massive in his thin face.

'Howay, Tommy, divvent cry,' Billy says, waking and jumping up. He crunches over the fallen stones to crouch down by him. 'You'll be in a better place soon with fields and grass . . . you'll get a holiday after this, you kna.'

I'd never thought about it properly before, when they told us at school how little kids worked in the mines. I didn't think of what a seven-year-old kid trapped in a mine would look like. Not a picture in a book, but a real little bairn crying his eyes out. One who should be in primary school or playing on the swings in the park, learning to ride a bike or hassling for a go on his big brother's Xbox.

'He's so little,' I say. I feel sick, knowing what I know.

'Nah – he's a big man, aren't you, Tommy?' Billy says, putting his arm round the kid. 'He's a trapper what sits in the dark and opens the traps – them's the doors that keep the fresh air goin' round, so we can all breathe. He's the youngest and the most important, aren't you, Tommy?'

The little lad nods, his black-smeared face showing white tracks of tears.

'I was a trapper once – best job in the world, eh? Gets you used to sittin' in the dark, gannin nowhere. Proper trainin'!'

Tommy gives a weak laugh and leans up against Billy.

'You come down here when you were only seven?' I say. I don't so much see Billy nod as feel the movement of his body.

'I was with me da. I was scared, mostly of the noise but then sometimes it would gan quiet and I'd think – they've all gone, they've forgot about me. And that's worse than the noise. But they never did. And you get used to it, don't you, Tommy? Me little brother, he was a trapper, but now he's a driver.'

'I'd like to do that, drive the ponies,' Tommy says. 'Better taking the wagons up and down them roads than sittin' in the dark. I gan and stroke the ponies when I can, but there's lots missing. Did the others get out, d'you think?'

Billy shrugs. 'I divvent kna, Tommy. I hope they did, and some of the lads with them. You go and get me fiddle from the ledge over there and I'll play you whatever song you like.'

Tommy gets up and trots into the darkness towards the sound of the men's voices.

'Is your brother here as well as you and your dad?' I say. I almost cannet bear to hear his answer.

'No, and I thank God he's not. He had the sweats that last morning we were up top. He was sick as a dog so I had a nap and some food and come straight back down. Took a double shift to cover for him. I'm a driver, n'all. Whatever happens at least Mam'll have one of us left to work and look after 'er.'

'So, you shouldn't even be here,' I say.

'Ah, who knows? Who can fathom the ways of things?'

Tommy comes back with the fiddle, but the lad with the tin box says he's finished it. He's so proud. We all pass it round and say good things and admire his scratched words to his mam.

'I give you that tin,' says one of the men. 'You've done a canny job there, like, son.'

The lad hands it to me.

'Fret not, dear mother,' I make out. His writing is wobbly and hard to read, scratched into the lid of the small tin. 'We were singing while we had time and praising God.' I feel sick as I remember Billy saying that they needed the fiddle – Granda's fiddle – resting now in Billy's hands.

'You're a reet professor, Will,' one old guy says. 'Look at that writin'!' They all nod.

'We've bin to the Sunday school,' Billy whispers in me ear, 'and the Methodist minister taught us to read and to write. But the older men never got much learnin', mebbe just their name. Some just make their mark, like a cross or a scribble.' Billy's so close to me I can feel the warmth of his body and see the strange grey tattoos on his skin. I guess he must really stink, but I cannet smell it. I figure me nose has got used to it and I must stink, n'all.

Will puts his little tin in his pocket. 'Mebbe there'll be the sound of the picks tomorrow and I can give it to Mam meself,' he says.

He seems quite cheerful now and says he'll take a bit of meat. The little kid, Tommy, has stopped crying and chooses a song that Billy whirls through, playing fast and furious as the men roar out the words. After a while, the playing slides into sadder, gentler tunes until the notes fade away. Then there's just the sound of a few men stumbling about and passing out chunks of raw meat. I can smell the metallic tang of blood and the stink of something goin' bad. I'm hungry, but not enough to eat that yet. Billy wraps the fiddle in some rags and cradles it like a baby.

One of the older men sidles up to him, holds his arm and whispers something. They stand there, sniffing like dogs, their blackened faces frowning – white sweat lines in the dirt. I realise that alarm is spreading through the group. One of the men jumps up swearing and another shouts, 'Lord, save us!'

'Lads, it's the afterdamp!' someone yells.

A woof of sound, a wave of heat and pressure hits us. I gasp for breath. There's an iron band round me lungs – I cannet get air. Every time I try, I drag in fumes that burn me throat.

I cry out 'Mam! Granda!' but nobody hears me. Billy's thin, strong hand drops down from me shoulder and he rolls on to the floor, coughing and gasping.

The last of the candles go out.

23

They stagger down an alley with water up round their ankles, gushing over the cobbles and cascading off the hillside.

'It's like climbing down a waterfall,' Deela says. Archie's pale face lolls over Mr Akthar's shoulder.

Kyle plods behind still clutching the empty fiddle case, the rain bouncing off his head. He points at a sign on an old brick warehouse painted black. 'The studio – over there!'

'Ring the police!' Mr Akthar roars as they crash in through the blue doors. A girl with short hair and a nose ring jumps to her feet.

'What happened? Is that Archie?' she says in disbelief.

'Ring the police and an ambulance! He's been attacked!' Mr Akthar shouts again.

Fogg comes out of a door and bellows, 'What?' He runs over to help, shock on his face. 'Get a blanket, warm him up. What's happened? Is he breathing? Mel, ring nine-nine-nine and get that first aid kit.'

A skinny lad with a goatee comes out of the studio, looking confused. 'Mr Fogg, are you coming back in to finish the session?'

Everyone ignores him.

Deela grabs the blanket off the old sofa and Mr Akthar puts Archie carefully down on the floor.

'Archie!' Deela whispers, as the men try to bundle him into the blanket.

Kyle kneels next to him. 'Archie, man, I'm sorry.' He shakes the water off his head. 'You're right, Deela, some bodyguard, me. I thought he was dead. Hold on, Archie, man, please. Divvent die on us.'

Archie coughs and turns his face. Deela touches his neck and he is so, so cold.

'We should get him dry. It's no good just wrapping him wet,' she says.

Fogg nods and starts to strip Archie right down to his pants, like it doesn't matter if everyone sees him stark naked.

'Woah, hang on!' Kyle says. 'Keep his dignity, man!'

Fogg's mouth gives a twitch of a smile. 'Better warm and alive than dignified and dead!'

They wrap Archie in the blanket and roll him into the recovery position. Fogg gently feels Archie's head. His fingers come away dark with sticky blood.

'This is bad.'

Mel hovers with some antiseptic wipes and a white wound dressing. 'I'll put this on for now. I think he might need stitches, though.'

'Who did this? Where did you find him?'
Fogg says. 'Is that his fiddle you've got there?'

Kyle looks up, ready to tackle the barrage
of questions, but Mr Akthar says firmly, 'He's
my daughter's friend.' He glances at Deela,
crouched beside Archie. 'We came to find
him. My daughter, she actually heard the
attack. She was speaking to him on her
mobile when it happened. We come down
straight away but the storm – *foof!* The roads
like rivers, the hill like a waterfall! I had to
leave my car—'

'But what *happened* to him?' Fogg says.
'Why would someone attack a nice lad like
Archie?'

Kyle sighs. 'Long story. There's these
twins – the Robsons. They've been giving us
grief. They must've followed him and beaten
him up. And nicked his fiddle,' Kyle points to
the case, dumped and dripping by the door.
'I found it, but it's empty.'

'Animals!' Fogg shouts. 'Worse than
animals! No respect for owt! That lad's got
talent!'

'Like it's OK to kill someone with no talent?' Deela whispers to Kyle, but she knows what he means. She picks up Archie's clothes, heavy with flood water, his T-shirt stained with blood. 'He's been through hell,' she says.

'And after you've got an ambulance, call the police,' Fogg continues. 'We've had a load of trouble down in the Valley these last few months. We've got to make a stand!'

Mel's standing by the window, phone to her ear. Her voice rises. 'What do you mean? This *is* an emergency! A lad's been attacked here!'

The tall guy with the goatee reappears from the studio with his guitar case in his hand. 'I'm just, like, gonna go,' he says. 'Can I have a free replacement session? I mean, this one's not really gone the way I expected . . .'

'Aye, fine,' Fogg says, frowning.

'You might have to swim,' Mel says. She comes round from the desk, shaking her head. 'They're saying an ambulance'll be at least an hour. It's chaos, you could tell they were in a meltdown. Trouble all over the city – roads closed, flooded, people hurt. I said he was unconscious and they asked was he breathing OK, and when I said he was they said could we try to bring him in ourselves.'

'And what would they have said if you'd told them he wasn't?' Fogg asks.

'They were gonna talk us through CPR. It's like the city's collapsed!' Mel says. 'Utter dystopia.'

Deela groans and watches the guy with the goatee and the guitar case stand at the door and peer out. He swears as he sees the torrent of water washing down the hill, a new river – dark and frothing, full of logs and rubbish and junk – heading towards the actual riverbed. A bicycle churns past followed by a wheelie bin with its lid flapping.

'Look at that! Just look at it!' Mel says.

Fogg smiles at the skinny bloke. 'Well, looks like you're staying, mate. Tell you what, put that guitar case down, put the kettle on and make yourself useful. Then I'll give you a free session another day.'

Deela gently touches Archie's hand and bends to whisper, 'Come on Archie, wake up.' Kyle is slumped by his feet, shivering.

Fogg watches Archie carefully. 'His breathing's a bit easier. I think he's coming round, thank God. We'll warm him up and in a bit we can get him seen by a doctor. It's a crying shame about that ambulance but, realistically, we'd be better off with a lifeboat anyway.'

Mr Akthar nods his head. 'If we can manage to carry him up the hill, to my car, I'll get him to the hospital myself. It will be quicker than waiting for an ambulance that never comes. Unless my car's been swept away.' He's not joking.

'What if you move him and it kills him?' Deela says. 'What if he's injured so bad and we make it worse? I know the bleeding's stopped, but we dunno what damage they've done to his brain.'

No one has an answer.

There's the sound of the kettle boiling and the wind outside, trees thrashing about, things banging. A swirl of air pushes into the room.

Mel is back at her desk, fiddling with her computer. 'The roads are, like, gridlocked. Cars just floating in the water . . . Woah! See this!' she says with a gasp. She flips her screen round to show lightning flashes striking the Tyne Bridge. It's on a loop. Each time there's the gasp and scream of the person filming. It looks like special effects – only it isn't.

Kyle goes over to the computer. 'Awesome!' he mutters, leaning over the desk.

'They will have to shut the bridge,' Mr Akthar says. 'Someone will have to check it is safe to use. That will cause a lot of problems for the city. Financial too.'

Deela looks, but she can't think about the city, only about Archie.

'Never seen a storm like it,' Fogg says in his big booming voice. 'Lightning hitting the

Tyne Bridge! Who'd have thought we'd live to see this!'

Mel and the guy with the goatee hand round mugs of tea.

'Lots of sugar,' Fogg says. 'For the shock.'

Kyle gulps his down, his teeth chattering on the rim. Deela sips. The hot liquid is amazing. She hadn't realised how cold she'd got, soaked to the skin. Mr Akthar tries to get a mouthful of warm sugary tea into Archie who coughs and splutters and doesn't open his eyes.

Deela holds on to his hand and whispers, 'Archie, come back . . . Granda's waiting on you. Your mam's waiting as well, come back.' She doesn't know why but she feels like he's lost in a dark place, and if only he can hear their voices he'll fight to come back. 'Granda needs you. He's calling for you.'

She gently touches his face, which is side on in the recovery position. His skin is pale and cool, but not the death-like cold of when they first found him. She notices for the first time the ridge of his cheekbone and how dark his eyelashes are. His eyelids flicker. What if he wakes up and finds her stroking his face like he's a cat? Awkward.

'Mam! Granda!' He calls suddenly and sits up. He groans and then throws up on the floor.

'Urgh,' Deela says. 'Thank God you're awake!'

Kyle pushes forward, holding the empty case. Deela motions with her head, trying to thought-transfer to Kyle to back off and hide it – now's *not* the time to talk about that.

'They nicked your fiddle, Arch!' he says. 'I saw them, the Robsons, they were legging it up the hill just before the lightning struck. They dropped the case. I saved it, but—'

'It doesn't matter,' Deela cuts Kyle off, rolling her eyes at him and pushing the case behind her. 'Archie, it's you that matters now.'

Mel gets a cloth and a bucket of water and starts to mop up the sick, looking like she's going to add to it any minute. 'I get all the best jobs! You feel better now? D'you want some water?'

Archie stares round, confused. 'Where am I?' He tries to focus on the faces. 'Deela? Kyle?' he stares at Mr Akthar. 'Where am I?' He puts his hand up to his head and winces. 'What's this? It hurts.'

'A bandage,' Kyle says. 'It's not surprising. Your head's a proper mess.' He helps pull Archie up slightly so he's half-sitting, half-leaning against Deela.

'Thirsty,' Archie murmurs.

Fogg gets some water in a mug and Archie gulps it down like he's never drunk before.

'Go easy,' Fogg says, but Archie ignores him. He stares at them like they're ghosts.

'Where are the others? I've got to get back. They need help!' he says suddenly, clutching his head. 'They're down the mine and they're trapped . . . I've seen them! They need help or they'll die.' He tries to get to his feet.

Fogg gently pushes him back down. 'Lie still and rest for a bit – no one's going anywhere yet. You've had a right crack on the head, haven't you?' His voice is a warm rumble.

'I know it sounds unreal,' Archie says shakily, between gulps, 'but I've seen them. He came to help me – that Billy who we met in the park.' His eyes are glazed, sleepy. 'You saw him, Kyle, you were there! And Billy helped me fight off them Robsons. They wanted me fiddle but he caught it when they threw it and then there was the lightning and something hit me.' He stops talking, puzzled himself. 'Oh, I dunno . . . but he led me down the mine. If you go in the tunnel you can get into it, only there's no way out!' Even as he says all this the rest of them can see his brain is struggling with how ridiculous it is. If you can go in through the tunnel then you can come out through the tunnel. He shakes his head.

'That tunnel doesn't lead into a mine,' says Fogg gently. 'It never did. It was an underground wagon way for taking the coal down to the Tyne. It went under the buildings, down to the river. I did that tour they run. The mine workings were much deeper. It's the bang on the head, Archie, it's got you all confused.'

Archie stares hard at the faces gathered round him.

'I found you just inside the tunnel,' Kyle says. 'It was flooding bad.'

'But . . . but I was in the mine . . . deep under the ground, I swear I was. Don't ask me how.' Archie puts his fingers to his head again, frowns as he feels the dressing stuck on the back of his skull. 'It's not just in me mind, I swear. I was *with* them. I thought I'd had it, that I was gonna die down there.' He stares at everyone around him. Fogg shakes his head and Deela scrunches up closer to Archie. 'An' if you can pull *me* out alive, mebbe there's a chance we can save them too!'

'It's OK,' Mel says. 'Don't try to think too hard, just give your brain a rest.'

'No!' Archie says again. 'Billy was down there. He went into the tunnel and he led me down there. Deela . . . Kyle . . . you met him! We've got to help him!'

'If anyone went into the tunnel they were probably just using it to shelter from the rain,' Fogg says reassuringly.

Deela says, 'When me and Archie were talking on the phone, before . . .' she hesitates, starts again. 'Archie said there was a group of tourists . . . but there was definitely nobody there when we got to him. He was in the mouth of the tunnel and the water was flooding in so deep he would've drowned if Kyle hadn't held his head up.'

Mel says, 'Listen! No thunder and lightning for ten minutes now. Maybe the storm's nearly over. So, if there was anyone down there, they'll be fine, right?'

Mr Akthar shrugs his shoulders. 'Some storms, they go round in big circles and there is calm at the centre. I think we're at the heart of the circle but it will come back round. We should get away as soon as we can.'

Fogg goes to the window and stares out at the flooded hillside, the rain drumming on metal roofs and the wind thrashing the trees about. 'The eye of the storm, it's called. My Gran used to say anything can happen in the eye of the storm.'

'I didn't know that was an actual thing,' Kyle says.

Archie's mouth moves and they bend closer to hear him.

'Can you hear the lads singing?' Archie says.

Everyone freezes for a moment, straining to hear. Is that noise in the distance singing? Or just the wind, moaning through the buildings?

There's a sudden flash so bright that the image of Archie sitting on the floor and Deela crouched next to him is burned on to everyone's retinas.

'You spoke too soon, Mel,' Fogg says. 'Here it comes again.'

'No!' Kyle moans. 'When will it stop? This is just, like, the end of the world!'

Archie tries to pull himself up. 'Aye, it feels like that when you're trapped.'

24

They're all staring at me. I'm not making this up, I didn't just imagine it . . . I think. I *was* down in the mine and I saw them men and boys, smelt the stench of sweat and wee and raw meat, heard the pit ponies stamping in their stalls.

The lightning strikes again and all the lights flicker. I remember the fear and the weird woof of sound as all the candles went out and the air was sucked out of me lungs so I couldn't breathe. What had they called it? The afterdamp.

'We've got to find them,' I say but deep down I know it's too late, whatever we do. I feel the tears well up for a moment. Billy and

Will and little Tommy and the men. Dead. All dead.

'You rest,' Mr Akthar says. 'I will check. Anyone in the tunnel is probably as safe as anywhere, but I'll make sure they can get out. And I will see if we can get you safely up the hill. At least you are warm and dry here.'

He doesn't understand, I think.

'I'll come too. Mel, keep an eye on Archie,' Fogg says.

I watch as they go out of the door, Fogg pulling on a giant red waterproof. A guy with a guitar case follows them out. Everything's so confusing. What's Mr Akthar even doing here? Why's Deela here when she's grounded? It's like a weird dream where everyone you know is in the wrong place. Only I'm glad she's here, sitting right next to me.

'Kyle,' I say, but it's too complicated and me head hurts. I close me eyes and feel the ground roll and the sudden heat and the panic. 'I cannet breathe!'

'Course you can, it's OK, it's OK,' Kyle says, pushing the cup of water at me.

I take a sip. Me head's all over the place. I cannet work out how I got back to the studio. I remember trying to run back, but the Robsons blocked me. I have a flash of memory, one of them shouting, 'Don't do it, Bry' and then the pain and the fiddle flying up into the air. But Billy was there and he caught it – he has the fiddle, safe, down in the mine. Like a kid, tears are rolling down me face.

'Sorry,' I say. 'Sorry.' I want to tell them about Tommy who's only seven and who loves ponies, and Will who's scratched out a message for his mam who'll never see him alive again – this is massive. All them lads will die 'cos they already have. I'm two hundred years too late to save them. How can I even start to explain that?

The noise of the rain on the roof and the constant sound of thunder joins in with the pulsing pain in me head.

I try to get up from the floor, fighting off
the blankets and realise it's all I'm wearing –
or not, as I've let it drop. I grab the blanket
and clutch it round me.

'Whoa! Where's me clothes gone?' It really
is like one of them dreams where you're
walking through school in the buff.

'Divvent look, Deela! You might get an
eyeful,' Kyle shouts.

Deela says, 'I'm not looking! Everything
was soaking wet. We had to get you dry and
warm. But don't panic, Fogg sorted you out,
not me!'

I'm not sure that Fogg seeing me naked is
any comfort, but I'm blushing at the thought
Deela might have. It's not like it matters, but
it makes me feel weird.

Mel laughs. 'Keep your hair on, Archie,
Fogg's seen it all before – some of the bands
we've had through here are proper
exhibitionists. Hang on, I'll find you
something to wear. Got some old merch and
lost property here. It's amazing what people
leave behind.' She rummages in a grey metal

locker and pulls out a hoodie that looks big
enough for me, Kyle and Deela to camp out
in, and a whole pile of black T-shirts. They
all have names printed on them of bands
none of us have ever heard of.

'There you go,' she says. 'Take your pick.'

Kyle pulls off his wet top and puts on an
enormous T-shirt that comes to his knees. It
says *Jagger's Baby*. 'What'd'ya think? Cool?
Or not cool?'

Deela says, 'Who even are they?'

He throws one at me but I have to lie
down again because I feel sick. I grab the
blanket round me and breathe in, out, in, out
– me belly's heaving and rolling like I'm on a
boat.

'I'll help you, man,' Kyle says. Then looks
at Mel and says, 'What about, you know,
trousers?'

'Funny thing, people leave all sorts of stuff
but not usually their trousers. You'll just have
to put your wet jeans back on, Archie.'

'You'll still be drier than the rest of us,' Deela says.

Kyle holds up a T-shirt that says *Stuff It – the tour!* And throws it at her. 'Go on – Mel says we can help ourselves. Cannet look a freebie in the mouth.'

'Ahh, that well known saying,' Deela says sarcastically, throwing it back. But she has a quick look through the pile, chooses one and goes off to the toilets to change. I shut me eyes. The swaying feeling's not so bad now. Kyle helps us get into some warm clothes and I slowly pull me jeans back on. They feel stiff and uncomfortable and remind me of being down the mine, the constant seep of the water coming out of the rock, sitting in the wet, sleeping in the wet.

There's a flurry of noise, the door swings open and a whoosh of wind sweeps in followed by Fogg and Mr Akthar. They have a man's body slung between them, his arms over their shoulders and his legs sort of hanging down. He's drenched through, the water sluicing off his bald head.

'Billy!' I shout, but it's not him. The man winces with pain. It's the old bald guy who was late for the tour group just before the Robsons turned up.

Fogg and Mr Akthar lower him on to the sofa at the back of the room.

'It's nothing,' the bald guy says. 'When we tried to come out of the tunnel the water was deep and I slipped. Twisted my ankle and there we were, stuck!'

'You can thank Archie,' Mr Akthar says. 'You were right, Archie, they've had some trouble getting out of that tunnel! I'll go and help the rest of them. Seems like there's no other injuries, but it's hard to see where it's safe to tread out there and some of them are not so spring chickens.'

Mel puts the kettle on again. 'Hope we've got enough milk,' she says. 'I'll ring and cancel that ambulance now Archie's back in the land of the living. How d'you feel, Archie?'

'Got a banging headache,' I say. 'But I'm OK.' I really want to go home and lie quiet, try to sort me thoughts. 'I'm fine,' I add. 'Really.'

Deela looks at me. 'Yeah, right. I don't think so.'

A trail of wet people start to come in. The woman with the clipboard appears, looking completely wired. 'What a nightmare!' she keeps saying. She takes the mug of tea Mel offers. 'What a lovely man that Mr Akthar is,' she adds. 'I tried to ring for help but there was literally no signal and it was hard to tell how deep that water was. And when Derek fell – nightmare!'

I close me eyes and let myself drift and it seems like only a minute before Deela's dad is back with the rest of the tour group. It's hard waking up. I think of Billy standing at the entrance to the tunnel. I can still taste the mine in me mouth. The past is now and Billy is here but not here. A heave of smell and sound swirls in me head. Billy said he'd look after the fiddle. He promised. I reach out for the case but it's empty.

Mr Akthar comes over and crouches down beside me.

'Did you go right to the end?' I say. 'There wasn't anyone else?'

He stares hard at me. 'No, there was no one else. Who else would there be?'

I sigh. I dunno what I was hoping for. Billy, standing there, waving the fiddle at Mr Akthar – that's what.

'You look a bit better,' he says. 'Not so greeny-grey. We should try to get you to the hospital – get you checked over – before you see your grandfather. No time to lose, Archie.'

Panic jolts through me. 'I've got to see Granda,' I say, remembering. 'I've got to explain to him about the fiddle! See, Billy and the lads, they needed it. I couldn't say no, could I? But he promised—'

'Woah,' Kyle says. 'Archie, it's OK. I mean, it's not OK, like not at all. I mean, you must be stressed to death over the fiddle. I know it's your best thing but at least you're alive, man.'

Deela is nodding along, looking like a really serious nodding dog. I want to laugh, but it turns into a snort and I taste sick in me mouth and swallow it down. *Eurgh*.

Fogg speaks, and it's so loud it kind of buzzes in me head and I have to close me eyes again. His voice washes over me like a wall of sound.

'We need to report what happened. Can you identify the lads who did it?'

'Tall red-headed lads,' Mr Akthar says, 'called Robson.'

'Those boys did this to you?' The tour guide woman sounds horrified. 'Oh no! I saw them. I actually saw them hanging about as I was coming down the hill. I thought they were waiting for a friend. That's terrible!'

It's all way too much noise and drama.

'Call us later, right?' Fogg says. 'Don't worry about your fiddle, we can get you another one. You get that head seen to first.'

Kyle's sitting hugging the old case like it's the coffin of his best mate. 'Granda'll be so sad when he hears,' he says, looking at me.

I think of the music Billy and me played down the mine that's as real as this room and these people. I think of the tune I learned that I hadn't known before, of me fiddle in Billy's hands and the way he played it.

'Granda'll understand. 'Specially when I tell him Billy needed it. One good turn and all that.'

Deela shakes her head, confused.

'It's where it needs be,' I say, hesitating. 'And Billy will look after it. He promised he'd not take his eyes off it.'

25

They've all got that look on their faces again.

'D'you think the Robsons have bashed his brain so bad he doesn't know what's real and what's not?' Deela says like I'm not even there.

Kyle shrugs. 'Nowt we can do about the fiddle, but we can get him to Granda – even if he's talking bat-crap.'

I want to say something sarcastic like, 'you met Billy, how can you say he's not real?' But I'm too tired to be bothered to even talk. I know we have to get going. I'm desperate to see Granda and Mam again but I cannet even lift myself off the floor, I'm that bone tired. Deela's dad hovers over us, touches me face. I open me eyes but I find it hard to focus on him. Mr Akthar says, 'The storm's easing off. Let's see if you can walk.' There's a silence as everyone judges me – and I obviously fail. 'And if you can't, I will carry you,' he adds. 'Kyle, Adila, ready?'

Kyle and Mr Akthar lift me up and put their arms under me armpits for support. The studio door bangs behind us and we're out into the rain again, Fogg's voice booming past, 'We'll meet again, Archie Bell!'

Deela says, 'How we gonna do this?'

'Easy,' Kyle says.

'Yeah,' she replies. 'We just have to wade miles through swirling dark water in the pouring rain. Dead easy.'

'Nah, man, divvent pass out again!' Kyle says, giving me a thump on me back. 'It freaks us out – you look like a zombie.'

'Sorry . . .' I'm trying to keep upright so I'm not just a dead weight hanging between them.

'You crying, Deela?' Kyle says after a bit and I open me eyes and try to turn to see. Deela's behind us and she shakes her head.

'No, it's just rain. On my face. Like, dripping down.'

Her dad says, 'You're doing good, Adila,' and sort of hoists me up again. Me feet start to drag and I think, I cannet do this. I feel like I'm in a washing machine, jolted and wet. In the end me legs just give way.

Mr Akthar stops and gets Kyle to help heft me on to his back. He just powers on through the muck and the rain, clambering up that slippery hill, his shoes sliding on the cobbles, but holding on to me tight. It's like he's waited all his life to be in this movie – Mr A the action man. Yesterday he was yelling at me. Today he's carrying me safe, back to Mam and Granda.

Kyle and Deela take turns to lug the empty fiddle box. I've closed my eyes so I won't be sick and mebbe they think I cannet hear them, but I can.

'What can we do about the fiddle?' Deela says. 'Granda's waiting for Archie, calling out for him, and he'll have to tell him it's gone. Even if the Robsons just dropped it, it'll be trashed by now – it's probably floated down the river.'

Kyle says, 'We just won't tell him – not yet. When he's better we can tell him. When he's out of hospital and he's got his scooter, when everything's back to normal. It's OK, we'll get Archie to his bedside and Granda will get better.'

'That's not going to work,' Deela says. 'First thing he'll ask is how the audition went. And d'you think he won't notice Archie's been done over? Don't you get it? Nothing'll ever be OK again.'

By the time we get up the hill the rain is slowing and there are more and more people around. Suddenly I see a guy in a boat rowing along the street, which is wild but he laughs. 'I've always wanted to do this! Hey, what's happened? Is he hurt bad?' He says he'll row us as far as he can until the water runs out.

Deela's dad heaves me into the boat. I
pull myself up but have to lean over the side
to be sick again. It's getting old but me belly
won't listen. Not that there's much to chuck,
just more acid and foul-tasting water. I spit
and try to rub me mouth.

Deela climbs into the boat and tries to
help me. 'Does your head hurt?'

What a question. It feels like I've got an
axe in it. 'Aye . . . and me eyes hurt. Me
belly hurts. Everything hurts. There was, like,
this sort of explosion and bad air. I couldn't
breathe.' I see her look at me, sort of pitying,
and I think, *she'll never get what happened.*

There's not room for the others in the
boat, so Mr Akthar and Kyle splash along
behind us, knee deep in water and half
pushing the boat along.

'I could be your, like, gondola,' Kyle says.
'If we were in – what's that place?
Amsterdam.'

'Venice,' Deela can't resist correcting. 'And
a gondola is the boat not the driver.'

'Sor-ree,' Kyle snipes back. 'I didn't know this was a *geography* lesson.' He dumps the fiddle case on top of her. 'You might as well hold this, save us carrying it.'

I look at her face. She's exhausted. There's a car in the distance, just kind of floating next to a trampoline, like some weird art installation.

'I'm just praying Dad's car'll be OK,' she says as we pass the wreckage. 'You can't be a taxi driver without a taxi, can you?'

Suddenly the boat scrapes on the road below and the guy says, 'End of the line! We can't go uphill with no water!' and I can see the wet tarmac stretching away and a huge traffic jam of cars, who've tried to come down the road but stopped where the flood starts.

'Woah, that's weird,' Kyle says. 'Is that steam coming off the tarmac?'

It's hard getting out of the boat. Me legs don't want to work. 'Please, just let me sleep.'

Deela says, 'What about Granda?' and I know I have to do it. Even if it hurts, you have to keep going, right?

Mr Akthar and Kyle grab an arm each and we stagger up the hill for a bit. There are huge puddles everywhere and the sound of water dripping and draining off into the soil. Rubbish and bins are just lying all over the streets, wherever the water took and dropped them. Kyle's shorter than me and Mr Akthar, so we're kind of lopsided as we climb towards our estate and the Spinney wood.

The clouds are lifting as fast as they came and the sun is hot on me back, the sky suddenly a bright blue. The tarmac's drying out, with steam rising and it looks like the road's smoking. You'd hardly know there'd even been a storm except the front gardens are all ponds and there's a heap of wheelie bins at the bottom of the hill. People from the abandoned cars on the coast road are wandering around aimlessly, asking for directions, and some from the estate are out as well, looking for the stuff the floods took.

'I lost me goldfish right out their pond! They just swam off down the garden path – carp with white splotches, if you see them.'

'Look out for the killer carp, Mr A,' Kyle whispers and Deela kind of snort-giggles. When we reach the Not-Library we stop and stare. There's a new lake where the grass should be and the blue sky and the trees are reflected.

'So pretty!' Deela says. 'Maybe it would be nice to always have a lake here.'

Suddenly I hear a shout. Gadget Guy's standing next to Tasha's white car, marooned in an enormous puddle. He comes striding across the mud and grass.

'You OK?' he says. 'What's happened to Archie? Have you ever seen anything like that storm?'

'The Tyne Bridge got struck by lightning,' Kyle says.

'Really? Wow! Tash's car is wrecked and we've lost two thousand pounds' worth of uni stuff.' He runs his hands through his hair. 'We put the ground radar equipment in the car, but we thought we might get a lightning strike in amongst all those trees so we made a dash for the Co-op. And while the end of the world was playing out, someone – some utter, total dopehead – broke a window and stole everything. It's not like it has resale value – there's not a huge market for hot image resonance equipment!' He looks frustrated, but his voice is mocking. 'S'pose I better just go and get a proper job and stop mucking around with digs and mapping and thinking I can be a real archaeologist.'

'I guess it couldn't be the Robson twins this time,' Deela says slowly. 'They beat Archie up down in the Ouseburn just before the storm broke. No way could they have got back up the hill that fast.'

Gadget Guy looks closer at me. 'Archie, you look like—' he glances at Mr Akthar, '—terrible. What did they do to you?'

'I dunno,' I say. My voice sounds tiny, pathetic. 'I was by the tunnel and . . .' I stop. I cannet get it straight in me head.

'By the tunnel?' he says. 'I live near there – right opposite. We've had a shedload of vandalism and trouble lately.'

Kyle hugs the empty fiddle case tighter. 'Aye, they stole his fiddle, just left the case. They'll take anything, them lads.' He thinks for a moment. 'Howay, man, they divvent need to have been here to take your stuff. It could be Tyler Richards or some of the other younger kids trying to get in with them.'

'Where's Tasha?' Deela asks, looking at the sad, flooded Mini.

'She's upset. She's just walked home. She was doing me a favour and now her car's a mess. I'm trying to phone the police to report the damage and the theft, but I can't get through.'

'You need a cup of tea,' Mr Akthar says. 'I'm taking Archie to the hospital, but Adila will take you all to ours. You go straight home now, Adila,' he adds. She starts to argue, but he says, 'Tell your mother we're all safe. Don't mention my car though.'

'What if she asks?'

'Tell her it's safe, too.'

'So, lie?'

'No, Deela, just tell her the truth that was the truth when we left the car. It was safe! She will worry and what's the point of meeting worry before she needs to? I can worry enough for us both.'

'Can I come to the hospital after?' she asks and her dad nods.

'Archie's mother is probably with Granda by now but if she's still at ours, tell her to come to the hospital quick.'

'I'll call her,' Kyle says, fiddling with his phone. 'I've finally got signal! She'll be off her head worried by now. D'you know your mam's number, Archie?'

I shake me head and it's like the whole world slides to one side and bangs into me skull.

Deela gives me an awkward, hard hug. 'You'll be OK now,' she says. 'Come on, Josh, let's calm Mam down and we can get dry.'

I watch her walk away with Gadget Guy, skirting round the new lake, heading for the alley and home.

I stand swaying, staring back down the hill. The place is chaos. Mr Akthar takes my arm again. 'Come on, last stretch. We can do this, Archie. Let's get to the hospital!' He gives a grunt as he hoists me up like a sack of potatoes, but I don't care. I lay me head down on his shoulder and close me eyes. It's like being a little kid again, getting carried home from a party by me dad. Before he turned into scum who left us all.

I can hear Mr Akthar's voice, a comforting drone, saying he's hoping a doctor will have a look at me, that he won't leave me till I'm with Mam. I let myself drift into sleep. It's a deep, comforting nothing for a long time.

And then the voices come. The men and the boys, the sad songs and the roaring ones where they stamp out the beat with their feet. Billy's leading them on Granda's fiddle, the tune high and clear.

I hear them singing us home to Granda.

26

Inside the hospital feels close and stuffy and there's that hospital smell that makes me feel sick again. I lean against a wall while Mr Akthar asks if someone can have a look at my head as I've been attacked.

'I'm sorry, this isn't an emergency unit. We don't take emergency patients,' a man says. 'You'll need to go across the city—'

'No ambulances, no transport – the roads are gridlocked,' Mr Akthar replies.

I slide down the wall, very slowly, so it supports my back. There is a silent standoff. Mr Akthar changes tack.

'The boy needs to see his grandfather. Mr William Bell? He's seriously ill and he's been

263

asking for him. Please can you tell me the ward number?'

The man looks confused. I realise what we must look like. Mr Akthar is soaked and filthy, and I'm wearing an enormous T-shirt and probably look like I've taken something I shouldn't have.

The man sighs. 'I'll get someone to have a look at him. But you'll still have to go to A and E for a scan.'

'I'll take him, as soon as the roads clear,' Mr Akthar promises, hauling me up.

'I think Mam's with Granda. I just want to see them, please,' I say.

And there she is.

She grabs me and hugs me and says, 'Archie, what's happened to you? I knew summat bad must've happened.' She tilts my head and stares into me eyes.

'Mam, *Mam* . . .' I hold on to her and feel her warmth and the grip of her arms. I smell her shampoo and deodorant and the underlying scent of her.

'Look at the state of you. We need to get you checked over.'

'No, I'm OK,' I say. 'Please, let me see Granda first?'

She gives me another tight hug. 'Love you, Archie Bell,' she murmurs.

'Love you, too,' I say. She'll probably never know just how much I mean it.

'OK, let's get you up there. He's been so unsettled, asking for you and for your dad and talking strange stuff about the fiddle.'

We all move along the corridor.

'It's a bit of luck you were coming past,' Deela's dad says.

'Not luck – Kyle rang us. Said you'd be bringing Archie and that he'd been hurt. I dunno how to thank you for getting him back to us,' she says.

At the big security doors into the ward, Mr Akthar stops.

'I'd best go home. Wash your hands and face before you see your grandfather, Archie.

And no silly talk.' He turns and walks away quickly, his shoes making a sloshing sound on the shiny floor of the corridor.

Inside the ward a nurse helps Mam clean me up, gently washing me face and hands. I explain what happened – the twins, the crash of something on to me head. The nurse looks me over and says to Mam, 'I think he's got mild concussion.' She takes a peek under the dressing. 'And he'll need a few stitches and a tetanus injection – you will take him to A and E won't you?'

Mam promises she will, as soon as I've seen Granda.

'And when the traffic goes,' I say. 'It's wild out there, so many queues and floods and,' I start to giggle, 'lost fish and flooded cars. Deela's dad had to abandon his. I was down the mine and Billy—' I stop. I'll have to learn to keep it to myself. 'And we came back in a boat.' I finish. It doesn't sound real, any of it. I try to think of the right words to say to Granda, about the fiddle and Billy. How to explain what I cannet explain.

The nurse goes to get us some water to drink. Mam's hands are shaking and I think she's crying but she's not, she's really angry.

'The state of your poor head,' she says. 'When this is all over, I promise you them lads'll get what's coming to them.'

We go into the ward proper and Granda's in the bed by the window. He looks so small and grey. He's got an oxygen mask over his face and his eyes are closed. Mam pushes me down into the chair next to the bed.

'Archie's here, Granda,' she says in a loud, fake-happy voice. 'He's a bit late because of the storm, it's been terrible out there!' She motions to the dressing stuck on the back of me head and shakes hers. I wasn't going to tell him anyway.

'I'm here,' I say. 'Sorry I'm late, but I'm here now.'

His eyes open and he suddenly grins and it's him again.

'Better . . . late . . . than . . . never,' he says between gasps.

I reach for his hand, buried in a fold of the blanket, but instead I touch something smooth. I look down, not able to believe it and yet so wanting to. I lift the blanket slowly.

There on the bed, close to his hands, is the fiddle.

27

Granda grips me hand and I wait for him to
say something, but he doesn't. He goes to
sleep and I listen to his harsh breaths. I find
myself trying to breathe with him, for him.
After about an hour, I look up and see Deela,
her mam and Kyle lurking at the ward
entrance. They're talking to the nurse and
Mam goes over to see if they can come in.
Deela's mam gives my mam a hug and a
picnic bag. Everybody queues up to use the
antiseptic gel from little containers on the
walls so the old gadgies on the ward won't
catch any bugs off visitors and Kyle sticks
some on his head like he's pretending to gel
his hair, but nobody laughs. I try to get up
from the chair, but they're quicker than me

and they're by the bed before I've heaved myself up.

'Thank you, Shazia,' Mam says. 'You didn't need to bring food.'

'You'll need something this evening and you'll be too tired to cook,' Deela's mam says.

'Honestly, I cannet thank you both enough. Our Archie's told us a bit about what happened.' Mam pauses and looks at Granda; he's still asleep but I swear his breathing's getting louder.

'Oh, Archie!' Deela's mam says. 'Your face is coming up all bruised – you're the colour of the storm cloud,' she adds. 'Proper purple!'

I try to grin, to show I'm OK.

'It was so good of Sarim to go after him in that terrible storm. Is he alright?' Mam carries on.

'Yes, he and Nabila have gone to find the car, we're just hoping it'll start. I'm glad you got to the hospital OK. I was worried you'd

270

all be washed away and I had no phone signal for any of you.'

'Aye, I ran as fast as I could – the water was up to me ankles.' Mam points to her feet, with no shoes, just some hospital socks on. 'But I didn't want Granda to be alone. I watched the storm out of the window.' She waves towards the view right across the city. 'Frightening. Like something out of a movie.'

Mam glances at the bed again and drops her voice low. 'I felt so helpless. Granda's so poorly, calling out and muttering, but he still knows us and knows we're here with him. He's settled more, now Archie's here. He does keep asking for Rob, you know, Archie's dad, but that cannet be helped. Getting Archie back in all this storm seemed like a wonder enough. And we cannet ask for too many miracles, can we?'

Deela's eyes fix on the fiddle, tucked into a fold of the blanket on Granda's bed. She looks at me, her eyebrows raised.

'Miracles?' she says. I know she's about to ask how the hell did I get the fiddle back, but at that moment Granda opens his eyes. His voice is very quiet and raspy, so we all lean forward to catch his words.

'Play . . . for . . . me, lad,' he says. 'It . . . eases the pain.'

I lift the fiddle, and the bow is next to it, just waiting for me hand.

Kyle's eyes are almost bugging out of his head. 'How did you get it back?'

I'm already tuning it up, twanging each string gently, listening, tightening the pegs.

Mam smiles and says, 'I'd just nipped to the loo so I didn't even see the lad who brought the fiddle up for us. Granda was restless, but the nurse was with him. She said some skinny lad came in, dripping wet, holding the fiddle.' She strokes Granda's hand. 'When I got back, there it was, on the bed! I think it comforts him to have it there.'

'But . . . who? *When?*' Deela asks, confused. Trying to work it all out logically.

'When the thunder stopped for a bit. We could hear some music – singing in the background – old songs, some programme on telly in another ward. I thought the storm was over. Then it all started up again.'

Kyle looks at Deela and me. 'Anything can happen in the eye of the storm,' he whispers.

I don't know what the rules are about playing the fiddle in a ward of sick old gadgies hooked up to tubes and machines, but I play a slow tune very quietly. Granda smiles.

'Singin' me home,' he whispers and closes his eyes again. The noise of his breathing fades. Deela jumps up and turns to her mam, but her mam shakes her head.

'Just dozing,' she says.

I pluck the strings softly and the sound hangs in the air.

'You'll get better now, won't you?' Kyle says to Granda. 'You listen on and you'll be out of here in no time.'

Mam gently tucks the blanket round him and quietly chats to Mrs Akthar.

'Archie,' Deela says, her voice low. 'Who brought the fiddle here? How did you get it back off them Robsons? What's going on? None of this is . . . normal.'

'I knew it'd be safe. Billy promised me he'd never let his eyes off it.' I trace each dent and scratch on the old fiddle, think how all the hands that've ever touched it have left a mark.

'But who *is* Billy?' Kyle says. 'You even called me Billy when I saw you lyin' on the ground. You looked up and said Billy.' He's frowning, like I betrayed him or something.

'You met him,' I say. 'Remember that lad in the park, the one who told us Granda needed us?'

But before they can ask any more questions I can't answer, a nurse comes in. At first, I think she's going to get radgy with us for playing the fiddle, which I guess is probably high on the 'not allowed' list. But she goes straight to Mam and says, 'We've had a phone call from a Mr Rob Bell. He says he's Mr Bell's son and that there's been a message on the radio for him to contact us. He's left a number – do you want to give him a ring?'

Mam's mouth drops open in surprise and she looks so like a fish, kind of gasping for air, that me and Deela and Kyle all start to laugh.

'How?' She says. 'Who would've put that on the radio? I certainly didn't.' She starts rummaging in her bag, looking for her phone. In the end she just tips everything on the floor, she's in such a hurry, and picks it out of the mess of lipstick and tissues and old receipts. Then she leans over Granda and whispers, 'He's comin', Billy. Your Rob's comin'. Just you hold on, pet.'

She rushes out into the corridor. Deela and her mam crouch down and pick up the stuff from Mam's handbag, pile it all back in. Granda starts coughing, so Deela's mam goes to get him a cup of water. But he still doesn't open his eyes.

I grin at Deela, though me cheek's sore when I smile. 'I just thought finding me dad would keep you busy, like, not bored,' I say. 'I should've known you'd sort it. D'you even know how clever you are, Deela? You're, like, the best, you kna?'

'Perhaps when he's back, you and him can, like, get to know each other?' she says.

Kyle looks away. He says, 'I need a drink, anybody want a can of Coke? There's a vending machine outside. Shall I get you one, Deela?' He stands up, pats his pockets. 'Got any money, Deela?'

'Just because Dad's coming to see Granda,' I tell him, 'doesn't make him any less of a scumbag. And it doesn't mean I'm gonna hang out with him.'

Kyle doesn't say anything, just goes off with Deela's cash.

'I guess it's all working out,' Deela says, but her eyes don't meet mine and she keeps looking at the fiddle like it's radioactive. I put it back on the bed and Granda's old hands, knotted and veined, rest against the wood.

'Does it matter?' I say. I'm so tired.

She puts out her hand to the fiddle just as I go to shift it so it doesn't slide off the bed, and our hands brush, but she doesn't move hers away. This little bubble of happiness comes up inside me. I sort of glance at her and she's blushing. For one moment our hands meet and clasp and then part as her mam comes back with a fresh jug of water for Granda.

We just sit for a while. It's so hot in the room, I feel like I'm floating. Kyle drifts back in, holding his can of Coke to his head like an icepack. He drops another on to Deela's lap. Finally, Mam comes in looking flustered.

'Rob's on his way,' she says. 'He's driving up the country, says he set off as soon as he heard the message and he's making good time. I've told him about the storm and he couldn't believe it. He says there's absolutely nowt down south, how strange is that? I told him it's gridlock here, but he says he'll find a way in.'

I try to put on a neutral face and luckily Mam isn't looking at me.

'When I was sending all them messages I just wanted it to be a happy ending,' Deela suddenly says. 'Except Granda's not getting better. How can that be part of a happy ending?'

'There aren't any endings,' I say. 'There's bad stuff and good stuff, but it just keeps on going without an ending, like a mule on a gin gan.' I laugh, remembering Billy said that.

'What's a gin gan?' she asks.

And then Granda, the still figure in the bed, gives a little raspy breath. 'It's a horse gannin round and round,' he whispers, 'turnin' a wheel . . . to pump the watter . . . out the pit.' He stops and we think he's finished, but he sucks up a gulp of air. 'Walk for days . . . in circles, them poor . . . workin' . . . horses.' Then he rasps again and gratefully sucks at a little water through a straw that Deela's mam is holding close to his mouth for him.

We sit, quiet, just waiting. I'm remembering all the stories, all the history Granda give us over the years, and how when there was a school trip everyone wanted to be in his group, even Kyle who says he hates history. *Especially* Kyle.

'The fiddle,' Granda whispers. 'It's yours now, Archie, lad . . . in the family . . . two hundred years. Found with his body . . . down the pit.'

A shiver goes through me.

'In the pit? Who was it?' I say, leaning closer to hear his voice, so faint and rasping. 'Was it your great-grandfather who had the fiddle?'

'Nah, he was just a bairn at the time . . . didn't gan down the mine that day. If he had, he'd be dead n'all . . . then there'd be no more of our family . . . no me, no Rob . . . and no you, Archie.'

I think about that. It's hard to imagine none of us being born, a whole family wiped out. Granda's voice rasps on.

'The fiddle belonged—' he stops to cough. I want him to stop talking, only I want him to keep talking. 'Fiddle was me great-granda's big brother's,' he whispers. 'A good player . . . and a good brother.' He coughs for what seems a long time, and Mam gently wipes his mouth with a tissue.

'Shhh now,' she says. But he carries on anyway.

'He took the extra shift . . . to give me great-granda a day off . . . Fever . . . No sick pay then, no hospitals.' He looks slowly at the oxygen machine, the old men propped up in the beds. He sucks in more oxygen from the mouthpiece. 'That's the story . . . His big brother took his place . . . and lost his life. Nobody knew why . . . he took the fiddle – bit strange . . . bringin' a fiddle down the mine . . . But one lad – they were alive down there, just trapped, see – he wrote down . . . they were singing . . . mebbes he somehow knew he'd need it.'

'Why didn't you tell us before?' Kyle says. He sounds almost angry. 'I thought you'd told us *all* the stories!'

Granda's voice is so low now, we can barely hear him. 'A dead man's fiddle. I thought yous were too young to know, Archie, it would turn you against it.' He paused. 'Your dad kicked against playing. But it's in our blood, that fiddle. In your blood.'

'What was his name?' Deela suddenly says, leaning forward to catch the sound of his voice. 'Your great-granda's brother who died in the mine?'

Granda starts to gasp and cough, and Mam hurries to put his oxygen mask back on.

I know before he says it.

'Billy,' he says. 'I was named for him . . . Billy Bell.'

28

Mr Akthar rings us to say some roads are still closed but he'll come and take us to A&E. I decide we'll leave the fiddle on the chair next to Granda, so he can see it and touch it if he wants to.

Mr Akthar's car's fine, which is good. It's a blur, crossing the city, but it reminds me of going with Granda in the ambulance. Seems a lifetime ago.

In the hospital we do a lot of waiting. Mam takes pictures on her phone of the state of my face. I don't want her to, but she says it's evidence. I go to the toilet and when I come back she's on the phone, her voice high and angry.

'Police,' she says after she's finished.
'They want us to go to the station and make
a complaint. A complaint! I told them we
were in the hospital and when we finish,
we'll gan back to be with your granda. If I'm
gonna spend hours in a waiting room, it'll be
at the hospital, not the police station. I've
told them about it, anyway. We can sort it out
later on. It's not right, like, is it?'

I have bright lights shone in me eyes. I
get rolled into a scan machine. Someone
gives me an injection and the pain slides
away. There's a buzz as they shave a bit of
me hair off, then I feel them tugging and
pulling as they clean and staple the wound.

'I thought you'd have stitches,' Mam says.
The nurse tells her staples are better.

I picture the staplers at school. At least I
can't feel owt. They give Mam a load of
instructions and a packet of painkillers for
me and tell her I'll have to come back in
tomorrow for them to keep an eye on me.

It's late when Mr Akthar drives us home.
Mam tucks me into bed like I'm about six

years old, sorting the pillows just right. She strokes me forehead. 'My poor bairn,' she says.

I go to sleep and there are no nightmares this time, just deep, deep sleep.

*

In the morning, I crawl out of bed with a stonking headache. I'm battered and bruised and I look like I've done a few rounds in a boxing ring. We go straight to see Granda. I'm dead worried in case he's got worse while we were away, but he's just the same, still breathing in that loud, heavy way. A nurse has come and done various things to make him more comfortable, she says. *Comfortable!* He doesn't look very comfy to me. The sun's shining and it's warm in the ward. I listen to his breathing and gradually I fall asleep in a chair next to his bed.

When I wake up, Granda's talking in his raspy old whisper and a man's bending over him, listening, holding on to his hand like he can save him from drowning.

It's Dad. I look at him. He's not as tall as Granda and he's dark haired, like me. I can see the sunlight shining off a patch on his head where his hair is starting to thin. He looks older than I remember him looking, and sort of tired and beaten down. But it's hard to feel sorry for him.

'Dad . . . Dad, I came as quick as I could,' he's saying.

His voice is choking up and I want to shout, 'Where were you? Why did you just leave us? What right have you to be here?' But then I see Granda's hand clinging to me dad's and I know Granda's pleased he's come. This is what he's been waiting for. I stand up and go and take Granda's other hand. Me dad looks at me.

'Hell, Archie. What's happened to your face, man?'

Granda moves his head anxiously, trying to dislodge the oxygen mask. Mam eases it away from his face and he whispers, 'Lads, lads . . . Stay together, lads and yous'll see the light . . . give us a tune, eh?' Just for a moment, his fingers grip mine with their old strength. With me free hand, I pick up the fiddle but only pluck one soft note so's not to disturb anyone else, just to let him know I've got it and it's all safe. And then I sing, very soft and quiet, the song Billy taught me, down in the no-star blackness as the water rose to meet us, as the dark came for us all.

And while I am singing, Granda stops gripping my hand and he stops doing the horrible rasping breathing.

And he dies.

29

It's like Billy said, there's never an end really
– life just keeps going round. But having to
keep going without Granda seemed a terrible
thing.

That first day after he'd gone, I didn't
know what to do with meself. I lay on my
bed, listening to the voices of Mam and Dad
downstairs. She made cups of tea and heated
up food that Deela's mam dropped off and I
thought, how can you be making plans to
bury Granda and at the same time cook and
eat and check the fridge for milk? After Dad
finally went off to stay with some mate of
his, she came into my room. I rolled over and
stared at the wall, waitin' for her to tell me
how I had to, like, deal with it. Only she
didn't. She just sat on my bed and didn't say

a word. After a while I sat up and she hugged me, her body shaking as she cried, dead quiet. But I couldn't cry.

I barely slept that night. Deela and Kyle sent a load of messages, but I didn't know what to say, so in the end I switched me phone off. I kept looking at the fiddle. It was mine now and I wished I'd never dreamed of the day it would be. I thought I'd never be able to play it again. But when I finally did sleep, I heard the music and the voices singing and I felt like he was there, close. I woke up and it was dead early, but I got up and went out anyway, down the Dene and to the Ouseburn. I watched the river rushing past like a silver thread, like the music winding its way through everything – Billy and the men in the dark listening to the fiddle and Granda saying 'play for me, it eases the pain.'

Me eyes went blurry as I stared up the valley. I blew me nose and went home, held the fiddle in me hands and put the bow to the strings.

Granda was right. It does help the pain.

30

I played at Granda's funeral, even though it was hard to make myself.

There was a good turnout with people from the estate who'd respected him. The Akthars were there, and Kyle and his mam too, only they were late and ended up at the back. Fogg came, with Mel and some others we didn't even recognise, people who'd known Granda when he was young and played music in the pubs. And us – me, Mam and Dad, looking like a family when we weren't. I made sure Mam sat between me and him, and I held the fiddle tight through it all. I stared straight ahead so I could pretend Granda was right next to me and when I went up to the front to play, I could almost hear his voice say, 'Howay, Archie, give us a tune.' I played some of his favourites and, even though I was scared I'd mess it up, I ended with Billy's song and I swear I felt like it wasn't just my fingers on the strings, but Billy's and Granda's n'all.

It was, like, the last thing I could do for him and I'm glad I did it. I could see my dad in the front row sobbing, but I didn't cry. I played like a pro and I kept thinking, *You did this, Granda, you gave me this. Dad didn't want it, but you gave it me instead. I know our history, I know it's in our blood, and I'm not scared of playin' in front of people any more.*

After, Fogg came over and swept me into a bear hug, me face up against his scratchy old black jacket. 'Your Granda would be proud,' he said and added, 'Come back to the studio when you're ready, Archie.' Which I wasn't. But he didn't forget us. He kept ringing Mam up and finally persuaded me to play at the studio with just him at first, and then the others. Now I'm down there all the time, rehearsing with the band, helping out and I'm learning to use the mixing desk n'all.

We've done some gigs that've all been good. Small venues, pubs and that. Fogg even put a recording of one of the songs out there and it's doing alright for a folk tune.

It's the song Billy taught us down the mine, in the dark. The one I played at Granda's funeral. Billy had called it the song the mams sing when they lose their bairns. People really like it, they write nice stuff on the website like, 'A long lost song, played straight from the heart.' Mam's dead proud and even me dad says he never realised this kind of music was still, like, a thing. I let people think Granda taught me – they'd not understand if I said I learned it off me great-great-great-granda's brother who died in a mine disaster two hundred years ago. If Deela and Kyle, who actually met Billy, cannet deal with it, how can I expect anybody else to?

But if music helped, nowt else did. School started back the day after the funeral and I was there in me uniform, wearing the same black trousers Mam got us for the service, looking normal. Only there was nowt normal. I couldn't concentrate and me head ached most days. Turns out them Robsons actually fractured me skull – nowt massive, like, just a tiny hairline fracture, and I didn't need an operation or anything, but no PE for months and the teachers treating me like I was made of glass.

Kyle took the whole bodyguard thing dead serious. Like, way too serious. Someone just had to look at me funny and he'd kick off. 'His brains could, like, spill out,' he'd say. 'One touch and he'll be dead. You want to be arrested like them Robsons? Nah? Then divvent touch Archie.' He tried charging a quid for people to look at me X-ray, but a hairline fracture's not that dramatic and word spread that it wasn't good value for money. Plus I got sick of the attention and Kyle not letting up on it all, like I was his new business plan. Then he started following Tyler Richards between lessons. 'Warning him,' he called it.

'He's younger and he's a puny runt and it looks like bullying,' Deela told him. 'Plus, it makes you late for every lesson.'

'So? No point gannin anyway, I'm not clever like you, you kna,' he said. 'Or "gifted and talented" like our Archie, the famous fiddle player.' He rolled his eyes. 'You'll be playing the Arena next.'

I didn't know why he was being such a divvy, but I knew what he meant about school – I wasn't sure there was much point in bein' there either. In those first few months I mostly just sat in class, staring out the window and thinking about all the things Granda could've been telling us that would be more interesting than quadratic equations and the names of the generals in the Vietnam War. When Kyle bothered to turn up, the teacher kept on at him, saying stuff like, 'You're *this* close to being put in the isolation unit,' holding her fingers so close you couldn't even get a sanction sheet slid between them.

Mostly I just felt too tired to think about anything, like I could sleep forever, only I couldn't sleep at all most nights. And when I did, I'd smell the mine or hear the voices and wake up sweating as the bottle crashed down, as the candles blew out. The police questioned the Robsons and, no surprise, first off they said they didn't do it. In the end, it was Gadget Guy that came through for us. He hassled his landlord to check the CCTV near his flat and sure enough, the twins were there on film, hanging about, one with a bottle in his hand.

It took months to get to court but I gave evidence on a video link, so I didn't even have to be there. I heard afterwards that Bry Robson had blamed his brother, only by then the bottle with my blood and Bry's fingerprints all over it had been found, stuck up a tree. Turns out, even identical twins have different prints. Granda would have been dead interested in all the forensics as he loved watching them telly programmes with CSIs in white paper suits crawling round crime scenes. Bry got two years in juvenile secure accommodation – or kiddy prison, as we call it – and Brad's back on the other side of the city living with his gran, doing some community programme to sort his life out. Gadget Guy even got some of his stuff back. Not the iPad, mind. And me and Deela stopped thinking about them and stopped bein' afraid to walk down our own street.

I was glad when it was over, like a weight lifting, only things weren't good with me and Kyle. I know I was busy with rehearsals and gigs and that, but it was him who'd make excuses not to meet or who would ghost me if I bothered to message. After a bit I even stopped callin' for him before school, cos I got sick of getting detentions for being late when he wouldn't get up and open the door. When I heard he'd finally been excluded for a week, I went looking for him. I found him on the bridge across the Dene.

We stood, with the bright green treetops below and the sound of kids playing, just like we had on that day last summer, before everything kicked off. He looked pale, with purple smudges under his eyes.

'Kyle, what's happened, man? The way you're acting up—'

'Fake news, I didn't do owt,' he said. 'Anyways, what's it to do with you, *mate*?' He leaned on the metal railings of the bridge and started moaning on about how I'd betrayed him, how I'm *always* out, playing in a *band*, seeing me *dad*, like it's a crime. 'Mates should stick together but you wouldn't know what that even means.' His voice was hard and didn't sound like Kyle any more. 'I thought you was like me, like we was brothers, only you're, like, so up yourself now, and I'm just . . . nothing.'

'If Granda was here, he'd be tellin' you to be man enough to ask school for a second chance.'

'Aye, but he's not here, is he?'

I turned away and stared out, over the park. It seemed like forever since I'd lost Granda. And now I was losing Kyle n'all. I shrugged, too tired to argue. There was a long silence.

'Sorry,' he said, his voice small. 'Only . . . do you ever, like, see him? Just gannin round a corner or summat. But when you get closer, turns out it's not him? I kna he wasn't like, me actual granda . . .' he stopped.

I looked at him. His face was red, screwed up tight.

'Only I miss him too, you kna,' he finished.

I grabbed his arm as he turned to walk away.

Two lads with no words, hugging on a bridge.

31

Loads of people tell you that things get easier after someone dies, like one day you'll just forget. But I still miss Granda so much sometimes I just want to crawl into bed, pull the covers over me head and never get up again.

Only, Granda wouldn't like that. He'd say, 'Howay, Archie, man, get up. Gan out and get some fresh air. Grab your life and live it! Not hide from it.'

So I keep getting up and life just keeps getting on and suddenly it's summer again with the park full of green leaves and flowers and today we're celebrating. I'm sat in the Civic Centre, with Mam and Deela and her family, and Kyle and Kyle's mam. Even me dad's here. We're all dressed up, smart, looking a fair bit different to the day of the flood.

The place is packed with people who've been nominated for community awards this last year, plus all their friends and family. The room's like a palace, with dark red carpets your feet sink into and sparkly glass chandeliers. The mayor's standing on a little stage talking to the audience and we're all dead quiet as the names are called: Sarim Akthar, Adila Akthar, Kyle Johnson.

Deela's mam's face is shining with pride. 'That's my husband,' she murmurs to a woman sitting near her. 'And my daughter. And her friend. They saved a boy's life in the floods, and helped a woman and her little children, and some people trapped in a tunnel!'

I sort of hunch up, embarrassed. It was only nine months ago, but it feels like a distant memory now of me sliding down into the darkness with the trapped men I couldn't save. I wonder how would it have been if Kyle hadn't held me head above water? If Mr

Akthar hadn't carried me to the studio and got me warm? If he hadn't helped me all the way to Granda's bedside, to be with him at the end? Mam's sitting next to me, in her best black trousers and high heel boots. She reaches out and touches me hand. I daresn't look at her or we'll set each other off bawling.

Deela goes up on stage and she looks so tall and elegant, her long dark hair in a loose bun. She collects her certificate. I already know what it says as I was there when Mr Akthar opened the letter telling him they'd all won an award: 'For people who have gone above and beyond in serving their community'. He was so shocked. 'What is above and beyond?' he'd said. 'I would do it again in a heartbeat.' Now he's smiling nervously as he follows Deela on to the stage.

Kyle's there too, a bit further behind. He's grown a bit these last few months and though he's still shorter than me and Deela, he doesn't look like a little kid any more. He's looking good in a borrowed dinner jacket with his diamond stud earring flashing under the lights. He hesitates like he's going to turn and sit back down again, as if he still doesn't think he deserves this. I see him touch his wrist, fiddling with a shiny watch that's a bit big for him and then he grins and keeps going.

It was Granda's watch. Me and Mam decided he should be the one to have it, cos he needed something of Granda's, just like I have the fiddle. Something to hold on to when it feels like the world's dissolving. Mam told him how Granda thought of him as his second grandson and would've wanted him to have his watch to remember him by – and so did we. Since then, Kyle seems happier. He's coming to school more regular and tries really hard not to kick off.

Mr Akthar turns back and grabs his hand, taking Deela's with the other. He lifts their arms up in the air and at that moment they look like rock stars, taking a bow as everybody else claps. They're all grinning, and I stand up and clap harder than everyone else in the room put together.

After, there are speeches and photos and
big trays of food laid out on long tables –
triangle sandwiches, little puff pastry things
with creamy fillings, chocolate muffins and
mini samosas that Kyle says aren't anywhere
near as good as Mrs Akthar's. Nabila's
stalking around taking loads of pictures with
a proper big camera she's borrowed from
college. She's got her mam and dad posed,
holding up the certificate, in front of a vase
of pink flowers. Deela's at the food table
chatting and laughing with Mam, and Kyle's
backed the mayor into a corner, trying to
persuade him to support the citizenship
group project at school so that people can
borrow a mobility scooter if they need it. I
can hear Kyle's voice, loud and enthusiastic.

'See, we just need a room to keep the
scooter in,' he's saying, waving his hands
around, 'only it's got to be, like, no rent or
dead cheap. What about in the Not-Library?'
The mayor's nodding, making encouraging
noises and Kyle's mam stands next to them,
gulping down a plastic cup of wine, looking
at Kyle dead proud, like she's only just
realised how great he is.

This is happy, I think. *Here, now. Even though we're missing someone.*

The truth is, I don't really know if we ought to be happy. But then, Granda never wanted us to be sad, did he?

I lean against one of the big windows and look out at the city and its people, walking past, getting off buses, sitting in the sun by the flower beds. Under the blossom trees there's a man with white hair, watching a skinny, scruffy-looking lad swinging on a branch. He twists and drops to the grass. I squint to try to see more clearly, but the sun's too bright. I close my eyes, just for a moment, and when I look again, they're walking away together, side by side past the flower beds and the bus stop, merging with the crowd.

Mebbe it isn't Granda, just some old gadgie who looks like him.

And mebbe it isn't Billy.

But I reckon it is.

Glossary

After damp: bad air with poisonous gases that could kill miners, as it was hard to detect.

Bairn: a child.

Canny: good / lovely.

Cannet: can't

Clamming: starving.

Divvent: don't.

Gadgie: a man.

Gan: to go.

Gan canny: go well / take care / good luck.

Gan yem: go home.

Gan radge: become angry.

Granda: grandad (da said 'dar').

Haddaway: no way / I don't believe you.

Hacky look: a dirty or angry look.

Howay: come on / get on with it. It can be used positively or negatively.

Hoy it: throw it.

Kna' ('nar'): know.

Lad: a boy.

Lass: a girl.

Mam: mum.

Man: used in the same way as 'mate' but also used to add emphasis to a phrase e.g. 'howay man'. Used for all genders.

Marra: a close friend (an old-fashioned word not used much by younger people).

Nee bother: no bother.

Nebby: nosy / too curious.

Pit / colliery: coal mines. The miners were often called pitmen or colliers.

Radgie / in a radge: annoyed / angry.

Up a height: in a strop / annoyed / upset.

Spinney: small woodland.

Wagons/Waggons: big carts of coal pushed on waggonways to the river (sometimes running through tunnels and under towns). These were first pushed by women and children, later by ponies and engines.

Wye aye, man: yes, of course.

You'll get wrang: you'll be in trouble.

Acknowledgements

The mining disaster in the story really happened. But all the people in this book are fictional, apart from one. Will, who scratched a message for his mam on a tin, was a real boy who lived and died in 1815.

I would like to thank the many people who've made this book possible:

My family, for encouragement, questions, music and all the times they've come with me to places that inspire stories.

Benton Park Primary School for taking us on a school trip to find out about the mining disaster in Heaton.

The staff at the Mining Institute, Newcastle upon Tyne, for bringing the past alive.

The people I've worked with, for all that's been shared.

New Writing North, who support new writers and help us keep dreaming.

Simon, Trevor, Ben, John and Roz of the Gosforth Writers Group, who encourage me to send work out.

And finally, the fantastic team at Hachette, including my wonderful editor, Jadene Squires, Jen Bowden for dialect support and Hannah Peck for the book cover of my dreams.

And to you, the reader. I hope you like it.

Author Photograph © Jon Forster

Karon Alderman is the New Writing North x Hachette 2022 winner, and is based in Newcastle with her husband, four children and assorted pets. Prior to this, her brilliant children's fiction writing won the Northern Promise Award 2012, and came runner-up in the 2010 Frances Lincoln Diverse Fiction Award. She currently teaches English and creative writing and is the Special Educational Needs Coordinator at Newcastle City Learning.